"God, Skylar, I can't stand the idea of never being able to see her again."

Skylar didn't have to ask who he was talking about. She could feel a weight spreading out like icy fingers in her chest as she put herself in his place.

"Would you like a minute?"

"No," he answered in a deadly quiet voice. "What I would like is to somehow get a lifetime back." He turned to look at Skylar. "Carrie's lifetime."

His dark tone undulated through her. "With all my heart," she whispered, "I really wish that I could give you that." She sighed. "But I can't."

"I know," he replied. He hadn't meant to insinuate that she could.

Skylar shifted in her seat, her eyes all but boring into him. "But what I can give you is my solemn promise that I will get this guy who did this to your sister—and to you—no matter how long it takes."

He looked at her then, her words hitting him dead center. She wasn't just paying lip service, saying the right things. "You mean that, don't you?"

Dear Reader,

I sincerely hope that by the time you get to read this letter, the words in it will no longer apply. The world will no longer be in a holding pattern and we will all be able to go on with our lives once again, well and happy. Not just because my son, Nik, and lovely daughter-in-law, Melany, have added another little soul to its number, but because the world had turned into a healthier, happier and upbeat place—despite the fact that my newest Cavanaugh book involves a serial killer whose world revolves entirely around himself.

The hero of the book is Cody Cassidy, a deputy sheriff from New Mexico. Cody makes his way to Aurora, California, where his twin sister, Carrie, moved to nine months ago. He hasn't heard from Carrie in several months and Cody cannot shake the feeling that something is very wrong. His path crosses with Detective Skylar Cavanaugh, who is determined to help Cody find out what happened to his twin sister. Their quest has them encountering victims and a highly unusual serial killer out to line his own pockets. In the end, he gets what he deserves. Come find out just how and I hope this story winds up entertaining you.

As always, thank you for reading one of my books and from the bottom of my heart, I wish you someone to love who loves you back!

With love and gratitude,

Marie Ferrarella

CAVANAUGH JUSTICE: UP CLOSE AND DEADLY

Marie Ferrarella

HARLEQUIN

ROMANTIC
SUSPENSE

Recycling programs
for this product may
not exist in your area.

ISBN-13: 978-1-335-73807-3

Cavanaugh Justice: Up Close and Deadly

Copyright © 2022 by Marie Rydzynski-Ferrarella

For questions and comments about the quality of this book,
please contact us at CustomerService@Harlequin.com.

Harlequin Enterprises ULC
22 Adelaide St. West, 41st Floor
Toronto, Ontario M5H 4E3, Canada
www.Harlequin.com

Printed in U.S.A.

USA TODAY bestselling and RITA® Award–winning author **Marie Ferrarella** has written more than three hundred books for Harlequin, some under the name Marie Nicole. Her romances are beloved by fans worldwide. Visit her website, marieferrarella.com.

Books by Marie Ferrarella

Harlequin Romantic Suspense

Cavanaugh Justice

Visit the Author Profile page at Harlequin.com for more titles.

To

Autumn Ferrarella

Welcome to the world, Little One!

All my love,

G-Mama

Prologue

The tightness in his stomach slammed into him when his second call in as many days to his twin sister went to voice mail. The tightness in his stomach coupled with the overall dark feeling that descended.

Something was definitely wrong.

Deputy Sheriff Cody Cassidy could feel it. Feel it all the way down his spine.

There were some who believed the myth of mental empathy between twins was just that. A myth. Well, they were welcome to their beliefs, Cody thought, but that didn't change anything that he knew in his heart to be true. He and his twin sister, Carrie, had always had this unspoken mental empathy between them.

It wasn't as if they lived in each other's pocket. Since she had moved away, sometimes weeks would go by before they talked—but they *always* talked sooner or later. Usually sooner than later.

However it had been almost two months now. Almost two months and *nothing*. Not a word, not an email or a postcard, or even a simple text message in response from Carrie.

Nothing.

He could have put up with that if it wasn't for the uneasy feeling undulating through him that something was off, something was wrong. And that uneasy feeling was growing stronger with each passing day.

Granted, he would be the first to admit that he hadn't taken Carrie's move out to Aurora, California, nine months ago all that well. But he *had* kept his misgivings to himself. Out loud he had told his twin to follow her dreams and that, no matter what happened, he would always be there for her.

At the very least, he had expected Carrie to keep in touch.

After all, Carrie had always been the sensible one, the one who had laid out her entire life for herself from the time she had been a very little girl. He had been the wild teen, drinking and carousing with his friends from early on, incurring her sad disapproval.

No one had been more surprised—and pleased— than Carrie when he had actually graduated college and gone on to become a sheriff's deputy—like their father before him—in the little town of Kiowa, New Mexico, where he and Carrie had grown up. He, Carrie had told him proudly on the day he graduated, had finally gotten his act together. That was also the day she'd told him that she felt it was finally safe for her to leave town, to explore her own options to see what life had to offer her.

Once, she had felt that she'd had everything mapped out, but now, she'd confessed, she was not so sure. Maybe there were other directions for her to go in, other choices for her to make. Maybe her earlier choices had been too rigid for her.

Cody had told her that he felt she could be anything she wanted to be, to reach for the sky. The world was at her feet and completely wide open.

Maybe that was it, Cody reasoned, staring at the phone on his desk. Maybe she was just too busy sampling life to be bothered to pick up the phone.

Or call him back.

She had always been the responsible one. When their mother had had cancer, Carrie was the one who had dutifully come home after school every day to take care of Alice Cassidy, never complaining that she was being deprived of doing what all her friends were doing: having a good time. Instead, she'd claimed that when her mother had finally gotten well, that was truly the greatest day of her life. Cody knew that Carrie had really meant it.

His sister's selfless behavior had been enough for Cody to straighten up and fly right, he reflected ruefully. Carrie had *always* been everyone's shining example. Her positive outlook had been enough to get their father to view life in a brighter light and pull himself out of his own depression.

Carrie had always had the power to heighten everyone's outlook.

And now, Cody thought with a sigh, he couldn't get her to pick up the phone—or return a phone call.

Dropping the old-fashioned receiver into its cradle, he terminated the call that never had a chance to get started.

"Problem?" Sheriff Matt Holden asked, genuinely interested as he passed by Cody's desk.

Cody raised his wide shoulders and then let them drop again in an almost helpless gesture. "It's probably nothing."

"But?" Holden asked, studying the young man's chiseled, clean-shaven face.

"I can't reach my sister."

The sheriff was aware of the kind of bond that existed between the twins. He had known them since their early childhood.

He raised a graying eyebrow. "How long has it been?"

"Two months."

The sheriff frowned. "That doesn't sound like Carrie. Why don't you take some time off and take a trip to her new home? See if you can find out what's going on?" his father's long-time friend suggested. "There might be a new beau in the picture." As the father of four daughters of varying ages, Holden knew what that could be like. "It's been a while since you took some time off," he reminded Cody. "And there's really nothing happening here that requires your attention."

Cody nodded as his eyes met Holden's dark brown ones. "Thanks, Sheriff. I think I just might do that."

He would have thought that just the idea of going out to California to see Carrie would make him feel better.

But it didn't.

The knot in his stomach refused to lessen or go away.

Chapter 1

"Up and at 'em, Sky," Detective Skylar Cavanaugh's partner, Detective Beaumont Rio, announced as he walked into the Homicide Division's squad room at a fast clip. It was barely eight o'clock in the morning.

Bleary-eyed, Skylar looked over at the much-too-bright-sounding man she had been partnered with ever since she had been awarded her detective shield less than a year ago.

"Not until my coffee has had a chance to kick in and work its magic," she told Rio wearily. Served her right for staying out late last night and catching that movie, she silently lectured herself.

Holding the steaming mug of black coffee between her hands, Skylar took a long sip, relishing the way it coursed almost seductively through her veins.

Recently married, Rio's newly acquired wider waistline bore testimony to how well he was being fed since he had exchanged vows with Marsha, his wife of the last three months. But right now, he didn't appear to be thinking about the satisfying breakfast he had consumed less than an hour ago. It was obvious that Rio was eager to get at it.

"It" being the latest case.

Ever since his marriage, Skylar's partner had been almost myopically focused on working his way up the ladder. He was attempting to do something noteworthy to catch the Chief of Detectives' eye.

"No time for that, Sky," Rio told her, shifting from foot to foot. "Morrow called in that they found a floater just outside the city limits."

By "Morrow," Skylar knew he was probably referring to Sergeant Jeff Morrow. Part of the Homicide Division for more years than anyone could actually remember, the sergeant was like the proverbial bloodhound when it came to finding bodies.

"A floater," she repeated after taking one last sip of her coffee and setting the mug aside. "Homicide or accidental?" she asked as she opened the first drawer on the left and took out her handgun. Very carefully, Skylar tucked the weapon into her shoulder holster.

"I actually asked him that," Rio answered, pleased with himself for anticipating his partner's question. "Morrow said it was too soon to tell. There didn't seem to be any telltale signs of a homicide or any outward signs of a struggle having taken place," he said, echoing the sergeant's words. "Could just be a simple suicide."

Skylar looked at him, thinking of the last parent she had had to break the news to about the woman's son's overdose. It had taken her more than a couple of hours to calm the woman down. Sitting there and holding Helen Jason's hand had been a truly heartbreaking experience as far as she was concerned.

Skylar's expression and tone hardened ever so slightly. "There is no such thing as a 'simple' suicide, Rio. Every suicide has serious repercussions for someone other than the person who died."

"Sorry, I didn't mean to minimize the end effect," her partner apologized. The way he survived personally, she knew, was to divorce himself from the act.

"I know you didn't," Skylar admitted. She shouldn't have raised her voice like that. "I'm being too touchy," she acknowledged. Taking a breath, Skylar said, "If it does turn out to be suicide, I'm anticipating having to break the awful news to some heartbroken family member."

"That's part of the job," Rio returned matter-of-factly.

"It is," Skylar agreed, "but it still rips my heart out."

"I know, I know." Rio's voice softened. "You do realize that you're way too sensitive for this kind of job, right?" he asked as they went to the elevator.

She looked at him, aware of the fact that a lot of the people who worked within the Homicide Division had self-made walls built up around them. It was a matter of survival. But those were the people who came across as too cold.

"Someone has to be," she told her partner. "Otherwise, we just become robots, working one case after another and going through the motions of being human."

Rio nodded. "I guess that's what makes us such a good team. Between the two of us, we wind up covering both ends of the spectrum."

Skylar absently shrugged her shoulders, wondering if maybe it was time for her to think about switching divisions. But if she did that, who would be left to feel empathy for the victim as well as for the victim's family?

Detective Beaumont Rio was a good guy, but she knew he just wasn't capable of that.

"You want to drive, or should I?" Skylar asked as they got off the elevator.

"Well, since you put it that way—me," he informed her with a big smile. "I'd like to drive."

Since she was still waiting for the coffee to kick in, Skylar decided it wasn't such a bad idea to let Rio get them to the lake. She had a tendency to drive too fast when she was agitated, and she knew it.

So did Rio.

"Be my guest," Skylar told him, waving a hand toward his aged beige vehicle. While it was reliable, it looked utterly uninspiring. The car was parked in its customary spot and she wondered how long that would remain to be the case.

Since his marriage, a lot of things had changed

in Rio's world. To be honest, she was surprised he was still driving the same lackluster car. She had seen him wistfully eyeing brand-new, far more colorful vehicles, and couldn't help musing that that was going to be the next thing to change in her partner's life.

Keep your mind on your work, Sky, she told herself.

At bottom, that was all that really mattered. The work, not Rio's quest for a flashy vehicle.

Getting in on the passenger side, Skylar strapped in.

"Did the sergeant give you any details about the floater?" she asked, since Rio was the one who'd caught the case. "Age, time of death, things like that?"

The vehicle came to life. Pulling out, Rio shook his head. "Other than the fact that a fisherman reeled her in and was totally freaked out by the event, no. I took the liberty of calling in the medical examiner and the crime scene investigation unit," he added, glancing at Skylar a bit nervously.

She saw no reason for the display of nerves on Rio's part. Something was up. "Are you waiting for me to bite your head off?" she asked.

"Well, I thought you might feel I was going over your head and usurping your position," he told her.

That had never come up before. For the first time, she found herself wondering if all was going well in Rio's marriage. At times, he had seemed rather preoccupied.

"Look, I know I'm related to more of the police

personnel than you are…" she began, only to have him laugh.

"More?" he echoed incredulously. "I'm not related to any of them. You, on the other hand—"

She didn't let him finish, especially since she knew what was coming. There were a great many Cavanaughs in different positions on the police force and, for some, she knew that could be a very intimidating fact. However, she had never thought Rio had fallen into that category. At least, he hadn't before he'd married.

"But what matters here," Skylar continued forcefully, "is that we're both homicide detectives with decent track records and good instincts. There's no reason for you to feel insecure."

"I'm not feeling insecure," Rio answered defensively.

"Good." Skylar nodded. "I'm glad to hear that, even though it was starting to sound that way. You shouldn't feel vulnerable," she reiterated, emphasizing, "especially since you did everything right." She was referring to his calling the CSI unit as well as the medical examiner to come on the scene.

"Sorry, Sky." Rio flushed. He was obviously uncomfortable with what he was about to confess. "Marsha and I had an argument this morning."

She knew what that meant. That was Rio's way of saying that his new wife was berating him. That sort of thing had started about a month ago. Skylar felt that Rio worked hard and he deserved a little peace and quiet, not a belittling or condescending attitude sent his way. That just wasn't right.

"If you need to talk," she told Rio, trying not to sound as if she was attempting to pry, "you know where to find me."

Rio had managed to arouse her curiosity, but she refrained from sounding as if there was any pressure in her voice.

Nonetheless, Skylar saw her partner's hands tighten on the steering wheel. For a moment, Rio seemed to be engaged in an internal argument with himself.

And then he finally said, "Marsha thinks that I should be higher up in my career by now than I am," he told her.

Her partner appeared embarrassed by what he was sharing with her.

She felt for Rio. She was also annoyed with her partner's wife for making him feel as if he was somehow failing her. If someone told her that it was none of her business, she would have countered with the fact that she felt her partner's mental well-being *was* her business.

Holding her tongue in check, Skylar merely reminded Rio, "Well, you are on the right path and, remember, slow and steady does eventually win the race."

"Apparently, not fast enough for Marsha," Rio muttered under his breath.

Skylar felt the same sort of protective feeling she experienced when it came to a member of her family dealing with some sort of slight. "Does Marsha have any idea just how good you are at your job?"

Rio stared straight ahead, deliberately avoiding her eyes. "Marsha doesn't think that accolades are very bankable."

That had to really sting. This was a side of her partner's new wife she hadn't been aware of until just now. A side she didn't much care for. But to be totally fair to the woman, maybe things were tighter monetarily than she was aware of.

Skylar told herself not to throw stones until she had more information, but it definitely wasn't easy to keep from speaking what was on her mind.

"Then you'll just have to show her otherwise," Skylar finally told him. She thought of something she had heard her grandfather say to one of her cousins. "You haven't been married all that long and there are always some rough spots to be experienced in the beginning," she told her partner. "My grandfather Seamus is fond of saying that the first hundred years are the hardest. After that," she concluded with a lop-sided smile, "it's all a breeze."

"A hundred years, huh?" Rio asked, taking the news harder than she thought he would. That caused her some serious concern.

Skylar nodded, flashing an even brighter smile at her partner. "That's what the man said."

"Well, between you and me," Rio confided far more seriously than she was happy about, "I don't think I'm going to make it."

"Aw, have a little faith in yourself, Rio. I know I do. Marsha just wants you to be the best that you can be," Skylar assured him, secretly hoping that she was right.

Judging by the expression on his face, Skylar decided that her partner was going to grasp that excuse she had just given him and hold on to it for dear life. She certainly couldn't blame him for that.

She was strongly tempted to talk to Marsha to make the woman see how her demeaning treatment was affecting Rio—even though she knew that she shouldn't be budding into her partner's life.

As they drew closer to the lake, Skylar saw the cluster of cars parked near the perimeter of the lake closest to their side.

Time to focus on the business at hand, Skylar told herself.

"Looks like the gang's all here," she commented.

Rio pulled their vehicle as close as possible to the crime scene unit's van without risking driving into the lake.

"Looks like we're the last ones to arrive at the scene," Rio noted. "We should have gotten an earlier start."

"Looks like," she agreed. Skylar looked around as they got out of the vehicle. There seemed to be officers everywhere. "Don't worry, I'll let Uncle Sean know that you get full credit."

"Uncle Sean" referred to the man who was the head of the Crime Scene Investigation Unit and the third of the older Cavanaugh brothers who had risen to a high-ranking position within the police force. There had been another older Cavanaugh brother, Mike, who, unlike all the other Cavanaughs of varying ages, hadn't been well regarded and had died while on duty.

Skylar had her suspicions about how the less-than-sterling officer had met his end within the ranks. Part of the known story was that, aside from his recognized two offspring, Patrick and Patience, he had fathered a set of triplets with a woman no one in the family had even known existed.

On her deathbed, she had told her children about who their father had been, as well as who they were related to.

Incensed that their mother had been so badly treated and that their existence had been virtually hidden, the triplets—Kyle, Greer and Ethan O'Brien—had descended on the Cavanaughs for a reckoning.

However, all had turned out well and shortly after the confrontation, all three had been taken into the fold and gone on to be part of the police force as well.

No matter what the difficulty turned out to be, Skylar reflected, things could always be worked out. The only thing that couldn't be smoothed over, she thought as she got her bearings, was death.

Along with Rio, she made her way over to the body of the extremely pale young woman who had been brought out of the lake.

The medical examiner, Marvin Edwards, began to cover the body with a sheet, then struggled to his feet.

"Definitely a younger man's game," Edwards muttered under his breath to no one in particular. His knees were likely bothering him again.

"If you were any younger, Doc, people would be accusing you of stealing your medical degree," Skylar teased with a wink.

With a groan, Edwards turned toward the familiar voice and then smiled. He enjoyed working with the young detective. "You catch this one, Skylar?"

"Rio and I did," she corrected, glancing at her partner. "What can you tell us about the time of death?"

The gray-haired man nodded a greeting at Skylar's partner. "Detective Rio," he acknowledged and then went on to answer Skylar's question. "Liver temperature puts time of death between five and seven hours ago."

That meant she had been asleep when this terrible thing was happening, Skylar realized. "What was the cause of death?" she prompted. "Was it deliberate, an accident, or—"

"Sky, I'm good, but I'm not that good," Edwards told her. "I need to perform an autopsy before I can answer that."

"Said he modestly," Skylar kidded. "Can you let me know as soon as you do determine the cause of death?" she asked.

"You'll be my first call," the ME promised. "Luckily, I don't have anything else on tap."

Edwards stood back and quietly sighed as his assistant, Walter, lifted the dead body and placed it on the gurney that would in turn be loaded into the ME's van.

"Time to get to work," he told Skylar as he went around to the front of the van and climbed into the driver's seat.

Chapter 2

As he got off the freeway and drove through the more urban area, Cody had to admit that he could easily see the allure of Aurora. It appeared to be, by all definitions, a very clean city, which he found rather amazing since it had been over fifty years that the one-time little town had incorporated. At last count, Aurora now had a great many more citizens within its borders.

According to what he had just read before beginning this odyssey, Aurora had all the advantages of a large city plus the heartwarming appeal of a small town, the kind where, at one point, everyone knew everyone else.

That truly wasn't the case anymore. Everyone *didn't* know everyone else, his sister had told him. But somehow, it still felt like a small town.

Cody felt part of the reason for that was strong infrastructure and maintenance. Any necessary repairs, be it to the buildings, the roads, or even trimming the trees, were immediately addressed and taken care of. The end result: everything looked neat and clean and completely up-to-date. Cody's own hometown, Kiowa, New Mexico, which at this point was a great deal smaller and older than Aurora, had the same kind of charm and efficiency.

Driving down the winding street on his way to Carrie's "apartment home"—a term he found amusingly quaint—Cody began to entertain the idea that if he couldn't get her to come back home with him, he might consider the idea of moving out here. After all, there was really not all that much keeping him in Kiowa now. His mother's cancer had resurfaced and she had died suddenly. Disheartened over his loss, his father had died shortly thereafter.

Lost in thought, Cody had driven right by Carrie's residential development. Realizing that he had passed it, he made a U-turn at the end of the long, winding block. He then circled back and pulled up into the cheerful-looking complex. Cody went on to park in one of the spaces labeled Visitor Parking.

The apartment home was not what he had come to expect. Bright and sunny-looking, the so-called "building" was only two stories high. The word *homey* instantly sprang to his mind as he looked at the structure.

It had Carrie written all over it, he couldn't help thinking—except, where was she?

Standing in front of her ground-floor apartment, Cody took out his phone and called his sister's number. Nothing rang in response. There wasn't even a message telling him that the call had gone to voicemail.

There was no response whatsoever.

Had she lost her phone or accidentally dropped it in water and it had gone dead? He recalled that Carrie always worried about short-circuiting her cell phone. She hadn't so far, but there was always a first time.

Well, he had come out all this way. He wasn't about to rent a motel room and sit there, twiddling his thumbs, until he finally got his sister on the phone. He needed to be *doing* something, not just taking up space.

Making up his mind about his next course of action, Cody headed for the rental office. Someone had to be there.

When he reached the front door, he tried it and found that it was unlocked.

The apartment manager, a sweet-faced, well-dressed older woman, looked up the moment she heard the door opening. Putting on a bright, warm smile, she looked over at him.

"Hello, may I help you with something?" she asked. "Are you interested in finding a new apartment home?"

Cody wasted no time. "Actually, I'm trying to locate my sister, Carrie Cassidy. She moved here nine months ago and she hasn't been answering her phone for a couple of months now. As far as I know, she still lives here, and I was hoping you could let me into her apartment." He saw the skeptical look in the woman's eyes and took out his wallet to prove that he was related to Carrie. His deputy badge was immediately visible.

But the badge wasn't the first thing that the woman behind the desk saw. She was looking at the picture on his driver's license and Carrie's photo beside it.

"I *thought* you looked familiar," she cried, pleased with herself. "Did anyone ever tell you that you look just like her? I mean with some differences, of course, but you really do look like your sister."

"Yes, ma'am," Cody responded. He didn't bother pointing out that he and Carrie were twins. Instead he said, "If you could unlock her door, I'd really appreciate it." He was hoping to find something in Carrie's apartment that would give him a clue as to his sister's current whereabouts.

The residential manager, Janice Miller, grasped the arms of her chair and pushed herself up to her feet. "Well, seeing as how you are her brother *and* a policeman to boot, I don't see why not."

Cody tried not to allow his impatience to surface, but it wasn't easy. There was a sense of urgency all but vibrating through him and he was having difficulty dealing with it. "Thank you."

"Of course," Mrs. Miller told him.

Stepping back, he gestured for the woman to lead the way, even though, because of the number on the door, he knew exactly where Carrie's apartment was located.

The rental manager paused by the small wooden boxes hanging on the wall. The boxes contained duplicates of the residents' apartment keys. Finding Carrie's key, she picked it up and then led the way out of the office.

"So, what do you think of our little complex?" Mrs. Miller asked cheerfully. "We've just finished renovating it—not that it was falling apart—but I always believe that staying a couple of steps ahead of the game is always better than hurrying to try to fix something that was beginning to fall apart."

She looked over her shoulder to see how the tall, blond-haired young man felt about her philosophy.

"Staying ahead of the game is always best," Cody responded, sensing the woman was looking for that sort of validation.

The bright smile the rental manager flashed confirmed his suspicions.

Carrie's ground-floor apartment wasn't located all that far from the rental office. Taking out the key she had pocketed, Janice Miller unlocked the door, pushed it open and then took a step back from the doorway.

"Ms. Cassidy?" she called out. "I have your brother here to see you."

There was no answer from inside the apartment. "Did your sister know that you were coming to see her?" the rental manager asked, looking at Cody.

The woman obviously didn't have a mind for retaining details, he thought, since he had already told her that he had called Carrie a number of times and hadn't gotten an answer. That was why he had come all the way out here in the first place.

"No, she didn't," Cody answered, keeping things simple.

"Well," she speculated, "she might have gone away on vacation."

Cody had begun making his way around the small, one-bedroom dwelling, looking for some indication of where Carrie could have gone on this so-called vacation. Nothing struck him. Her clothes were still neatly hung in her closet and her suitcase-on-wheels was standing in the corner. If she had gone on vacation, she hadn't taken anything with her.

"She wouldn't have gone away for any extended time without letting me know," he murmured more to himself than to the manager.

Mrs. Miller had a different opinion to offer. "Oh, I don't know. A woman in love can do impetuous things," she told Cody.

That stopped him cold and he turned to look at the woman. "In love?" he repeated. "My sister was in love?"

Since when? The question throbbed in Cody's head.

Janice Miller nodded. She looked very pleased with herself to be able to throw a little light on the situation. "I guess she didn't tell you."

"No," Cody said flatly, stunned at the news and still not altogether sure that it was true. "She didn't."

"Well, I hate to break it to you, but I guess you two aren't as close as you think you are," the rental manager told him.

"No," he quietly agreed for the time being, "I guess we're not. Did you happen to catch a glimpse of my sister's 'friend'?"

The woman looked a little indignant at the suggestion. "I have better things to do than spy on the people who live here," Mrs. Miller informed him. Then, after a moment, she relented. "I did see him leaving with her a few weeks ago. He was tall, muscular. " She smiled at the memory. "Good-looking."

Cody needed more details than that. "Hair?" he asked.

"Yes, he had hair."

Cody caught himself before the sigh could escape his lips. "What color was it?"

"Brown—I think," the woman answered after a beat had gone by. She sounded far from confident about her response.

All right, he thought, he had a color. He needed more. "Light brown? Dark brown? Straight? Curly? Long? Short? Thin? Thick?"

She shook her head, not in response to his question, but to clear up a misconception before she could even attempt to give him an answer. "I'm not sure."

This wasn't getting him anywhere. "Does she have any other friends here?" he asked the rental manager. He knew that Carrie hadn't mentioned any friends the last time they had talked. But then, she hadn't mentioned a boyfriend, either, but there obviously seemed to be one in the picture.

Mrs. Miller lifted her shoulders in a hapless gesture. "Not that I know of," the woman confessed.

Definitely not getting anywhere, he thought. It served no purpose to keep knocking his head against the wall. Cody took a card with his cell phone number on it out of his wallet and handed it to the rental manager.

"If you think of anything—or if my sister suddenly comes back—please give me a call," he requested.

Mrs. Miller took the card in her hand and looked it over. "I certainly will—Cody," she said, emphasizing his name with a smile. "Cody and Carrie." She nodded her head in approval. "That's cute."

"Our parents thought so," he told her.

During what had turned out to be his last conversation with his sister, Carrie had mentioned that she was in the process of looking for a new, more satisfying job. Since she had never gotten back to him about that, he felt that he only had one option currently open to him.

He needed to file a missing-persons report. "Could you point me toward your local police station?" he asked as he pocketed his wallet again.

Mrs. Miller suddenly became very somber. "Do you think something happened to your sister?" she asked. But even as the words came out of her mouth, she seemed to discount them. "Aurora is a very peaceful, law-abiding city."

Lord, I hope nothing's happened to her, Cody

thought in response to the woman's question. Out loud, he merely said, "I was always taught to cover all my bases."

Janice Miller nodded her head in agreement. "That makes sense."

She led the way out of Carrie's apartment and subsequently took Cody toward the residential development's entrance. There, she pointed to the cross street that was directly on her left.

"Just go out here and proceed about half a block to the left. The police station is right there, next to city hall. You can't really miss it," she told him, then added, "Unless, of course, you're driving with your eyes shut. In which case, the police will find you and bring you in," she guaranteed with a comical smile. "Good luck."

Standing on the edge of the sidewalk leading out of the development, the rental manager remained there with her arms crossed at her ample chest, watching as he drove away. "Good luck!" she called out again.

He hoped that it was just a matter of luck and nothing more. But that feeling that something was definitely off just continued to hover over him and intensify.

He told himself not to focus on the worst happening. He reasoned that there could be a dozen reasons why Carrie had decided to just disappear this way.

But for the life of him, he couldn't come up with a single one.

Maybe he could have if this wasn't Carrie, but it

was Carrie, and she had always been responsible to a fault. Even as a very little girl, she wouldn't have ever just taken off. She had always let her parents know where she was. Where *he* was as well.

Carrie had behaved like a little old lady from the very moment she could walk, he recalled. And this was in a little town where the population never went over thousand and where everyone not only knew everyone else, they also knew where everyone else *was*.

With all his heart, he wished he had said something to Carrie, had told her not to go. But he hadn't thought it was his place to stand in her way, especially since he had been such a typical wild child in his teen years, or at least, Kiowa's definition of a wild child at the time.

At the very least, he should have come out here with Carrie. But at the time, he was finally making something of himself, finally focusing on working hard and creating a career, one that he realized he had always wanted.

Turning into the police parking lot, he looked around for guest parking. Finding it, he parked his old car and got out, taking in the general area.

There were about twelve, fifteen, steps leading up to an official-looking building that was nestled next to a shorter structure. The latter was labeled City Hall.

Considering what they were supposed to be, the buildings both appeared rather homey-looking. But then, Cody reminded himself, things were not always what they seemed.

And even that went beyond for serial killers like Ted Bundy.

Cody felt his heart skip a beat. Where the hell had that come from, just out of the blue like that? he silently asked himself. Its origin completely eluded him.

No, it didn't, he thought the next moment. He was allowing his imagination to run away with him. Cody silently upbraided himself.

The simplest explanation was always the most applicable one, his father had always maintained. And Elliot Cassidy had had a great deal more experience on the job when it came to dealing with so called "bad guys" than Cody had when his father had finally retired his badge.

Standing in front of the police station entrance, Cody counted to ten, took a deep breath and told himself this was all going to turn out for the best. Only then did he pull open the glass door and walk in.

Cody just wished he could actually get himself to believe that.

Chapter 3

Preoccupied with the result of the autopsy she had just been privy to, Skylar was in the lobby, walking toward the elevator. Belatedly, she did a double-take after she was well past the front desk.

She could have sworn that the blond-haired man talking to Sergeant Elroy Phelps, the officer who usually worked the front desk, looked a great deal like the woman who had been fished out of the lake yesterday.

Except that he wasn't nearly as pale, Skylar observed. But pale or not, the man did appear to be rather distressed.

Curiosity had always been second nature for Skylar. It was actually the reason why she had initially become interested in what was referred to as the "family business" in the first place.

Unable to help herself, she drew closer to the front desk, trying to find out what the man was doing there. She probably would have just been on her way back to Homicide if the distraught-looking man in the worn, tan, fringed jacket hadn't reminded her of the woman who had just been autopsied.

"I need to file a missing-persons report," he was saying to the desk sergeant. "Could you tell me where I need to go or who I should speak to about that?"

That was all Skylar needed to hear. A couple of minutes ago, she'd been bracing herself to conduct a massive search to try to find the dead woman's name as well as attempting to locate some possible member of the deceased woman's family. Now it appeared that she would be spared having to go through all that.

But the man standing in front of the desk sergeant, asking to file a missing-persons report, would not be spared, in any sense of the word.

"I'll take it from here, Sergeant," Skylar told Phelps.

The sergeant instantly brightened. "Thanks. I'd appreciate that, Detective."

The man requesting to file a missing-persons report turned to look at the woman who had just spoken. She had to be part of the police force, he decided. It struck Cody that they had more police officers in Aurora than there were actual residents in all of Kiowa. Maybe he was worrying for no reason.

"If you don't mind my asking, what is your relationship to the person you want to file that report about?" Skylar asked.

By way of an answer, Cody took out his ID and held it up for the woman as he replied, "She's my sister. I'm Deputy Cody Cassidy with the Kiowa Sheriff's Office. Carrie moved here nine months ago. We're ordinarily very close," he went on to explain, "but I haven't heard from her in two months. My calls to her cell phone keep going to voice mail—except for the last call I made."

"Oh? What happened to that one?" Skylar asked, even though she had a suspicion she knew the answer to that.

"That one didn't even ring," Cody answered. He took a breath before continuing. He wasn't normally the type who shared things, but this was Carrie he was talking about. He knew that this edgy feeling he was experiencing wasn't about to go away until he found her. "She's a very dependable person and I'm worried that she's not calling me back because something might have happened to her."

Something had, Skylar thought, but for now, she kept that to herself in case the young woman the medical examiner had just performed his autopsy on did not turn out to be the deputy's sister.

"So, can you tell me where I can file that missing-persons report?" Cody asked when the woman he was talking to refrained from making any comment.

There were times when she hated her job, Skylar thought.

"Follow me, please, Deputy," she said, leading the way to the elevator.

She pressed the down button. When it arrived a moment later, Skylar walked in and waited until the deputy followed her. Once he was inside the elevator car, she pushed the button for the basement.

Cody looked at her curiously. "Your Missing Persons office is located in the basement?" he questioned.

With all her heart, she wished she could say yes, but she couldn't.

"Not exactly," she replied.

The same bad feeling, the one that had been his ever-present companion since he had come out here, looking for Carrie, reared its head and intensified.

And kept intensifying.

He found that he was having trouble breathing.

Cody glanced at the woman. "What's going on, Detective?" he asked. Belatedly, he recalled, "You never gave me your last name."

"It's Cavanaugh. Skylar Cavanaugh," she told him.

She was killing time and she knew it. Killing time so that she didn't have to say those dreadful words that could very well divorce the deputy from any source of hope. *I think we found your sister floating in the lake.*

For now, she kept that to herself.

"But you can call me Sky, if it makes you feel more comfortable," she told him.

Just then, the elevator reached its destination and the door opened. The path was well lit, but it still felt as if there was a lingering darkness about the area. A darkness that underscored and pervaded the bad feeling Cody was so acutely aware of.

He got the sense that the detective was stalling—and that made him nervous. "What aren't you telling me, Detective?" he asked her.

Skylar knew that she couldn't continue to beat around the bush this way. It wasn't fair to the deputy. Her eyes met his and she felt her heart begin to ache. "I'm afraid we found a body." She took a breath, bracing herself. "I need you to make an identification, Deputy," she told him quietly.

He didn't ask her any questions regarding why he was making this identification. Instead, he stoically followed the detective down the hallway to a room where he instinctively assumed autopsies were performed.

Pausing in front of the door, Skylar put her hand on the doorknob and then turned toward him and asked, "Are you ready?"

Am I ready?

Was anyone ever ready to have their whole life ripped apart and forever changed? he wondered.

His mouth was dry and his throat felt as if it was closing up on him, but standing out here wasn't going to change the ultimate outcome of what he was about to see.

Cody squared his shoulders then, nodding toward the door, said, "Open it."

Skylar had gone through the identification process a number of times before and it never got any easier.

Moving like someone trapped in a bad dream, she opened the door for the deputy and led the way in.

"We might have the victim's next of kin, Doc," she informed Edwards as she entered.

"Brother," Cody corrected, staring straight ahead at the form under the white sheet. "I'm her brother."

Skylar nodded. "My mistake. Her brother," she clarified respectfully for both the medical examiner and the deputy's benefit. "Doc, if you could please pull back the sheet so that Deputy Cassidy can make the proper identification," she requested.

"Of course," the older man replied in a subdued voice. He very carefully lifted the sheet away from the young woman's face.

Skylar was aware that the young man standing beside her instantly recognized the woman on the gurney. He stiffened as if every single bone in his body had suddenly gone rigid.

Cody stared at the lifeless body of his sister. For one awful moment, he felt as if his heart had completely stopped beating—and then suddenly launched into double time.

He hadn't expected this, not in any manner, shape or form. Even as he'd gotten off the elevator and begun walking toward the morgue, he had been hoping against hope that there had been some sort of a mistake made, that the person on the autopsy table would not turn out to be Carrie. Never mind that the dead woman was someone else's sister, or daughter, or significant other. Right now, he just selfishly wanted it *not* to be his sister.

But it was.

It was Carrie.

Taking in the wet hair, the pallor of her face, he felt tears stinging the corners of his eyes.

For the first time in his life, Cody was glad that his mother was no longer alive. This sort of thing would have surely killed her.

"Can I get you something to drink?"

The voice asking the question came to him from a distance, registering belatedly.

He forced himself to take a breath. "What you can get me," Cody told the detective with some difficulty, "is the name of the person who did this to my sister."

Every word felt as if it was sticking to his lips, to the roof of his mouth.

She knew that this was going to be difficult for him to hear, but he needed to know. "Right now, it looks as if your sister died by suicide," she told him.

The medical examiner moved forward and covered the dead woman's face. Skylar gently took the deputy's arm and tried to lead the victim's brother away.

Cody pulled his arm from her, the look on his face suddenly coming alive. His expression was animated.

"That's impossible," he almost shouted. "Carrie wouldn't do that. She was always the responsible one, the one everyone always turned to for guidance whenever something went wrong. Even me," he added quietly.

"The autopsy showed that she had a large amount

of fentanyl in her system," Skylar told him. She knew that this was difficult for him to hear, but he had to be told so that he could make peace with what had happened.

Cody balked. "That's not possible. She didn't believe in taking any drugs. My sister didn't even drink alcohol. When I was a teenager, she used to give me a hard time because I would go out drinking with my friends. She was the reason why I finally stopped drinking," he told the detective. Cody shook his head in adamant censure. "There has to be some mistake."

She pressed her lips together. There was more, and she dreaded telling him, but it needed to come out. "The autopsy showed that there was something else as well," Skylar told him.

Cody could feel himself growing almost icy cold. "What is it?"

"Your sister was pregnant when she died."

Stunned, Cody refused to believe what the detective was telling him. "Carrie wouldn't have killed herself and she definitely wouldn't have killed her baby. One of her dearest dreams was to one day become a mother."

"Maybe it happened sooner than she'd planned and things just got out of hand," Skylar suggested, "and she couldn't handle it."

He shook his head. "Even if the pregnancy happened unexpectedly, she wouldn't have done *anything* to terminate it, that just wasn't who she was," he told the detective.

"Was there anyone in the picture?" Skylar asked

the deputy. "Someone who could give you some insight into your sister's last days?"

Last days.

That sounded so painfully final, he thought. But then, that was what it was, wasn't it?

Final.

Carrie might be gone, but he was not about to buy into the scenario surrounding that event. His sister had *not* killed herself.

Cody tried to think, but it wasn't easy. All his thoughts felt completely jumbled up in his head as he struggled to make sense out of what he had just been told.

And then he grasped onto a thought. "The rental manager at the apartment complex where Carrie lived told me that my sister had a boyfriend."

"So you didn't know that she had a boyfriend until that point?" Skylar asked.

He let out a breath that fairly vibrated with the frustration he was experiencing. "No, I didn't."

Skylar nodded as she took in the information. "Well, first thing I need to do is to put a name to this so-called 'boyfriend.' If nothing else, at this point, the man is *definitely* a person of interest."

"We," Cody corrected. When the detective looked at him quizzically, he clarified. "The first thing *we* need to do is put a name to this 'boyfriend.'"

"No offense intended, Deputy, but I am already part of a very sharp investigative team," she told him, "and we'll be looking into this. It's our job."

Cody did not find that reassuring. "I either come

with you, Detective," he told her, "or I'm going to investigate this on my own." The words rang with finality. "And before you tell me I can't, I am part of law enforcement, same as you, and she is—*was*— my sister. I owe it to her to find out exactly what happened. So, I can either work with you, or on my own. The choice is up to you. And, for the record, there are no other choices on the table in this matter."

Skylar paused for a moment, considering him and pretty much knowing exactly what he had to be feeling. In his place, she would have felt exactly the same way until she was able to unravel everything.

A small smile rose to her lips. "There wouldn't be a Cavanaugh somewhere in your family tree, would there?" she asked.

He stared at her, highly confused. "Excuse me?"

"You're as stubborn as one of my brothers—or one of my cousins, for that matter," Skylar told him.

The deputy shook his head and looked exceedingly sad, in her estimation. "No, no relation. With Carrie gone, there's no one left but me."

Skylar looked up at him, feeling exceptionally distressed for the man.

"I am really terribly sorry for your loss, Deputy," she told him. "Those words hardly seem adequate, given what you are going through, but I am sorry about what happened to your sister, no matter how this has to sound."

He knew she was referring to the fact that she thought Carrie could have killed herself. But no matter what, no one would ever be able to convince him that Carrie had taken her own life.

Cody was certain he would have known that she had, *sensed* that she had. No, this had been done *to* her by someone else. Even though the detective felt that Carrie had ended her own life, he was confident that the drugs found in her system had somehow been given to her. Slipped into a drink or into her food.

He knew without a doubt that Carrie would have never taken those drugs willingly.

Cody would have sworn to that.

Chapter 4

"Why don't you come upstairs with me so we can plan your next move?" Skylar suggested. "If you're right and someone did slip that fentanyl into her system—"

"They did," Cody maintained firmly. As far as he was concerned, this was not up for debate.

She wasn't going to argue with him about that, not without proof. "Then this isn't going to be solved in a day or two," Skylar told him, leading the way to the elevator. "If you're really determined to work on your sister's case, do you have somewhere to stay?"

Cody shook his head as he followed the detective onto the elevator. He hadn't thought that far ahead. "I drove straight from Kiowa to my sister's apartment." He could feel his throat closing up again. "I was really hoping to find her there."

Well, that much made sense, she thought. "I know this has to sound indelicate, but do you know if your sister was paid up until the end of the month?" Skylar asked.

He hadn't asked the rental manager, but he was certain that was the case.

"Carrie was always very good about staying on top of her bills," he told her. "Why?"

"You could stay at her place, then," Skylar suggested. "It would give you somewhere to sleep and you could also use your waking hours to go through your sister's things, maybe you could find something with this so-called boyfriend's name on it to steer us in the right direction."

He really couldn't think clearly, he realized. Otherwise, that would have been the first thing to have occurred to him.

"I'll check with the rental manager," he told the detective, then decided to give her her due. "But that's not a bad idea."

Skylar smiled. "I don't have bad ideas," she told him. "Just occasional flashes of brilliance." She saw the dubious expression on his face. "I'm kidding. Sorry, I'm just trying to help you loosen up a little bit. Otherwise, you won't be able to deal with any of this because it'll all be much too oppressive for you."

The elevator came to a stop and he looked at her for a second before getting off. The detective meant well. He should have realized what she was saying. But he was just so anxious to get to the bottom of this, to find the person who was responsible for ending his sister's life, that he was having trouble focusing his thoughts.

He needed to get better control over himself. For Carrie's sake, if not his own.

"Why are we here exactly?" Cody asked Skylar when he realized that, according to the sign on the door, she had brought him up to the homicide squad room.

"Well, for one thing, the squad room might very well be a relaxed atmosphere, thanks to Lieutenant Anderson, but I still can't just take off when I want to. I have to tell the lieutenant that we have a name for the Lady in the Lake—that was the way we were referring to your sister," Skylar explained, suddenly thinking that maybe referring to his sister that way might have been a mistake.

Carrie, among other things had most recently been a substitute English teacher. A romantic at heart, she had always been partial to the Arthurian Legend.

Cody smiled sadly. "She would have liked that," he confided. "She always liked stories tied to King Arthur."

Skylar nodded her head. "Too bad I never got to meet her. I have a feeling we would have gotten along very well."

"Everyone got along with Carrie." And then, abruptly, he realized exactly what he was saying. "Well, almost everyone."

Skylar gave up thinking that this had been a suicide. Cody was too convinced that his sister wouldn't have done that and she tended to believe he was right. His sister had been murdered. The question remained why.

"We'll get him," she promised.

Cody appreciated the detective's reassurance, but there was one thing wrong with her theory.

"By Kiowa's standards, Aurora is a metropolis," he noted. "Finding the person who killed my sister could amount to the proverbial search for the needle in the haystack."

Skylar didn't want him growing despondent. He wouldn't be any use to her that way.

"We have an excellent track record here in Aurora for closing cases. If the guy has a pulse, we'll find him." Indicating her desk, she suggested, "Why don't you sit down and wait here? This shouldn't take too long."

There were framed photographs from one end of the desk to the other. The only other things on it was a laptop and a phone.

"Is this your desk?" he asked.

"It is," she answered.

His eyes swept over the framed photographs. "You do have a lot of photographs on your desk," he commented.

"I have a big family," she told him. Too late, Skylar realized her mistake. Right now, that was like rubbing salt into his wound. She wanted to apologize, but felt that might even make things worse, at least for now. So instead she just focused on the immediate job at hand—notifying Lieutenant Anderson. "I'll be right back," Skylar said as she quickly hurried away.

Left to his own devices and trying very hard not to think about what Carrie had to have gone through in her final hours, Cody studied the various faces that looked up at him from the framed photographs.

If this was her family, they appeared to all be rather good-looking, with similar features. He noticed there was one large group picture of a number of relatives of all ages.

She had an extremely large family, he caught himself thinking just before the wave of sorrow and emptiness swept over him. It made him that much more acutely aware of his loss.

He shook himself free of that sensation. He could grieve later. Right now he had to find that SOB and make him pay for stealing Carrie's life from her.

He didn't know what made him glance up just then, but he saw Skylar approaching him.

When she caught him looking in her direction, she beckoned. It was obvious that she wanted him to follow her to her superior's office.

"Lieutenant Anderson wants to meet you," she explained, then turned on her heel and led the way.

He could see that happening back in Kiowa, but here there just seemed to be too many people in the room for a meet-and-greet situation. And this was just one department. There were a lot of other sections within the Aurora police department.

Kiowa's entire police service consisted of four people—three deputies and the sheriff. And that was if he didn't count Shirley, the woman who worked the phones.

The lieutenant was on his feet even before Cody had a chance to cross the threshold into the man's office.

Extending his hand, Anderson immediately told the man with Skylar, "I'm sorry to hear about your loss, Deputy. Cavanaugh has pleaded your case and told me your qualifications," he said to the visiting law enforcement officer. "You are more than welcome to temporarily work with my people to find the scum who did this to your sister." It wasn't unusual to accept help from visiting law enforcement personnel.

Looking to Skylar, Anderson nodded at the young woman he had already labeled as a "go-getter" in his mind. "All I ask is that you keep me abreast of your progress." He smiled slightly. "You'll be in good hands with Cavanaugh being your guide, Deputy Cassidy."

"Thank you, sir," Cody said to the lieutenant, adding, "You can call me Cody, Lieutenant."

"All right, Cody," Anderson acknowledged. "Her partner, Detective Rio, will be joining you as well." The lieutenant glanced down at his watch. "Looks to me like he's running a little late—but he will be here," he promised. "Funny thing is that Cavanaugh here is the one who's always on time, if not early. Rio's the one who's mostly late these days. In the world I knew when I was a young guy, women were always the ones who were fashionably late," he recalled with a wistful expression.

And then he looked at Skylar. "I take it that Rio is still adjusting to the life of a newlywed, right, Cavanaugh?"

She thought of her last conversation with her partner yesterday morning, before the medical examiner had taken Cody's sister to the morgue.

"So he tells me," she answered her superior. She knew that Anderson loved to gossip. It was harmless gossip for the most part, but she had observed that those exchanges with Rio always seemed to pique the man's interest.

Just then there was a quick knock on the lieutenant's door and Rio stuck his head in before Anderson could invite the detective in to join them.

"You're looking for me, sir?" Skylar's partner asked.

"I am," the lieutenant answered. "Turns out that we have a name for that victim who was brought in yesterday."

"Really?" Rio asked, surprised that the case seemed to have progressed to this extent. He and Skylar hadn't had much time to dig into it yet, especially since they had spent most of yesterday tying up loose ends on another case. "Well, that had turned out to be lucky."

"Not for the victim," Skylar said, kicking Rio under the desk to keep him from saying anything further.

Rio's eyes widened as he glared at his partner accusingly. The warning expression in her eyes kept him from saying anything, or yelping in surprise.

Skylar indicated the other person in the room with her eyes.

The message was conveyed even before Cody said, "The victim is my sister." He couldn't get himself to use the past tense yet when referring to Carrie. It was still much too painful.

Rio instantly seemed chagrined because of his initial cavalier reference to the deceased. "Hey, I'm really sorry, sir. I meant no disrespect," he apologized in the next beat.

The lieutenant spoke to clear things up. "Deputy Cody Cassidy believes that his sister, Carrie—the young woman discovered yesterday at the lake—was the victim of a homicide. If that turns out to be the case, I need the two of you to find out who's responsible," he told Rio.

Casting a sympathetic glance toward the dead girl's brother, Rio nodded. "We'll do whatever we can, sir," he promised.

"No," Skylar said, speaking up. "We'll *do* it." She emphasized the word. Her look took in her partner as well as the deputy. "We have a damn fine track record when it comes to closing cases. There's no reason to believe that this investigation will go any differently."

The lieutenant nodded. "I agree." Looking at his detectives, he asked, "Does anyone have anything else to add?"

The three other people in the room shook their heads.

Satisfied, Lieutenant Anderson gestured to the

door. "Then go off and do me proud," he told his own two people. He went on to add, "If someone did kill your sister—"

"They did," Cody interjected firmly. There was no room for doubt in his tone. He was completely convinced that someone had killed Carrie. What he needed to do was to find out why and who, and he was not about to rest until he had those answers.

"Then Cavanaugh and Rio will find that person or persons," Anderson told Cody with finality. "Be sure to keep me up to date."

"You got it, sir," Skylar promised her superior.

Once all three of them had filed out of the lieutenant's office, Skylar immediately got down to business.

"Why don't we go and talk to that rental manager at your sister's apartment first?" she suggested.

Before Cody could make any sort of a reply— or Rio could ask his partner a question—Rio's cell phone rang. Pulling it out of his pocket, he frowned when he saw the number.

"I'm working right now, Marsha," he began impatiently, about to cut his wife off. And then, right before Skylar's eyes, Rio turned pale. "Where did it happen?" he asked, then queried, "When?"

Skylar recognized the fear in her partner's voice. She held her hand up, halting their progress out the squad room door as she took in the look on Rio's face.

"Where is she?" Rio asked. "All right," he said in a hollow voice. "I'll be right there."

The moment he ended the call, Skylar asked, "What happened?"

"It's Marsha. She was in a car accident," he said, his voice choking. "That was her sister on the phone."

Skylar didn't bother asking how bad the accident was. While she fervently hoped it wasn't serious, what mattered was that it had happened.

"Go," she told him. "Marsha needs to see you and you need to see her."

Rio looked from his partner to the man who had just lost his sister. He was torn between concern and what he felt was his duty. "But—"

"Go," Skylar ordered. "I can handle this end. Give Marsha my love—and call me as soon as you know that she's all right," she told Rio. Then she quickly hugged her partner before he could leave, promising Rio, "She's going to be all right."

The man nodded, clinging to his partner's words. Rather than take the elevator, he dashed over to the stairwell and took the stairs down to the first floor.

Observing it all, Cody looked at the woman beside him. "You want to go back to your lieutenant and ask him to assign someone else to accompany you?"

She looked at him, surprised by the suggestion. "I have someone else," she told him. Her eyes met his. "I have you."

"I meant someone from your squad," Cody clarified.

"I'm not prejudiced," she quipped, her lips curving. "Seems to me that you have more invested in finding the answers than anyone else does. Let's go—" she cast a glance in his direction "—unless you're uncomfortable working with a woman."

He thought of Carrie and, for just a moment, a fond smile bowed his mouth. "I was *born* working with a woman."

He reminded her of her brothers and the way they would have responded. Skylar was glad that the dead woman had had Cody in her life to care about her.

"Then let's go," she encouraged.

Chapter 5

Janice Miller looked up from what she was doing when she heard the office door open. The pasted-on smile turned genuine as soon as she recognized who had just walked in.

"You're back," Mrs. Miller noted, greeting Cody. "Did you find your sister?"

"I did," Cody answered, his voice extremely down-beat.

The rental manager looked at him, clearly confused. Her eyes shifted to the young woman with the deputy. "Is everything all right?"

Skylar answered the question before the woman could prod Cody any further. The faster she was informed of what had happened, the faster they could move this along.

"Ms. Cassidy was the victim of a homicide," she told the rental manager.

A look of disbelief crossed Mrs. Miller's face. Her hands flew up to her mouth as if she was physically trying to suppress the cry that rose to it.

She looked at Cody. "I am so sorry. Your sister was a lovely young girl," she told him, at a loss as to what else to say to the man.

"Was Ms. Cassidy's rent paid up until the end of the month?" Skylar asked, bringing the woman's attention away from Cody.

It took the manager a moment to think. "I believe so, but I would have to check," she told Skylar.

"Please do," Skylar requested.

"And you are?" the woman asked, looking at Skylar. It wasn't that she was looking for some sort of a confrontation, but she did need to know who this woman she was dealing with was, in the scheme of things.

Skylar took out her identification and her badge, holding it up as she answered Mrs. Miller's question. "I'm Detective Skylar Cavanaugh," she told the woman, further explaining, "I am looking into his sister's case for Deputy Cassidy."

"Of course, of course." The woman nodded her head. She hurried back to her computer to look up the current status on Carrie Cassidy's rent payments. Her fingers almost wound up knotting themselves together as she typed quickly, searching for the up-to-date information.

Finding what she was after, she glanced up and

announced, "She was paid up to the beginning of next month."

That was what Skylar was hoping to hear. It would make things a lot easier for Cody. "Would it be breaking any rental rules if Deputy Cassidy remained in his sister's apartment until the first of next month?" she asked. That date was almost three weeks away.

The question threw the rental manager. She hadn't been expecting that. She thought for a moment.

"I don't think that would be against any of the rules," Mrs. Miller told the detective, then asked her, "Would this have anything to do with your investigating who killed Ms. Cassidy?"

That was definitely part of it, Skylar thought. But there was more to it than that. However, she felt it was far simpler to merely go along with that excuse rather than to get into any further explanation for now.

"Yes," Skylar answered quickly for Cody.

He didn't want to stand there, answering the woman's questions about Carrie. He had his own questions that needed answering.

"Would you happen to know if my sister was close to anyone in this development? Or was she friendly with any of her neighbors?" he asked.

"Well, this is a very friendly place," the rental manager was quick to tell Cody. Then, in all honesty, she had to add, "But it's also rather a transient place. People here are in the middle of getting their lives set up. By that, I mean saving up to buy what they hope will be their permanent home, or at least close to being their permanent home," the manager explained. "You know, they're on their way from 'here' to 'there.' This just happens to be the stopping-off place in the middle."

Dissatisfied with the way she was conveying her point, Skylar gave it another try. "It's a little like striking up a conversation on the bus. You don't really remember having had it five minutes after you get off." She looked at Cody, feeling for him. "In other words," she concluded, "don't get your hopes up."

Skylar nodded, but she told the rental manager, "We'll still knock on some doors, if you don't mind."

Mrs. Miller gestured around the general area freely, urging, "Please, by all means, be my guest."

"She didn't sound very encouraging," Cody commented the moment they had walked out of the small rental office.

"Most people don't want to believe that they are anywhere near the presence of evil. It makes them feel vulnerable, as if they're not really safe," Skylar told him. "But at the same time, if we talk to your sister's neighbors, maybe someone observed something that might inadvertently point us in the right direction."

Cody looked at her, a bemused expression on his face as he shook his head.

"What?" she asked, unable to guess what he might be thinking.

"You are the strangest combination of optimism and pessimism I have ever encountered," he replied.

Skylar's eyes crinkled a little as she said, "I've been told that before. Thinking that way actually balances things out for me," she confessed. "That way, I'm not too dour about the crime I'm working, but I can still remain hopeful that I am growing close to the solution. I find that both attitudes are important when I'm working a crime."

He supposed that made sense, Cody thought. But right now, he just wanted to find someone who could tell him if they had seen his sister with the man who had gotten her pregnant.

He couldn't shake the feeling that whoever it was had the answer to what had happened to Carrie.

"How do you want to do this?" he asked Skylar, trying to curb his impatience. "Do you want to split up?"

She wasn't in favor of that. Under the circumstances, she didn't want to let him loose on his own, but she pretended to consider that idea.

"Well, that way we could cover twice as much ground," she agreed. "However, I've always found that two sets of eyes are better than one when looking at evidence."

Cody shifted from foot to foot. "So which is it?" he asked.

Her eyes met his. "I've always worked best with a partner," she told him. Her mind went to Rio. He hadn't called her yet. She really hoped that wasn't a bad sign.

"Well, I don't usually have that luxury," Cody told her, then admitted, "But then, we don't have that much crime in Kiowa, either." He looked at her. "So you get to choose."

Skylar inclined her head, silently thanking him. "We'll knock on the doors together."

There was no one home in the first three apartments they tried. The fourth and fifth apartment had someone at home, but they looked blankly at the photograph Cody held up for them.

"She kind of looks like you," the sixth woman at home in her apartment commented.

"That's because that's a picture of his twin." Skylar volunteered the information to spare Cody.

"Really? I always wanted to have a twin," the woman said, taking a second look at the image.

Skylar caught herself thinking the woman was not the brightest bulb in the box. She attempted to hurry the conversation along, although she didn't have much hope that it would yield anything.

"So you don't recognize her?" Skylar asked.

The woman shook her head. "I'm afraid not. But if you come in," she said, opening the door farther, "maybe something will come back to me."

By the expression in the woman's eyes, Skylar felt she could just guess what the woman was hoping would "come back" to her.

Skylar took out a card from her wallet and handed it to the woman.

"If anything does 'come back' to you," she said, emphasizing the sentiment, "give me a call. That's my cell phone number and that's my number at the police station."

The woman took the card, tucking it away in her pocket. She seemed rather disappointed to have things end so quickly.

"Maybe you were right," Cody told Skylar as they walked away from this last apartment.

"About…" Skylar prodded.

"About our not splitting up." He went down to the first level. "I got the very distinct impression that the last woman wanted me to 'step into her parlor.'"

Skylar smiled, well aware of the old saying about the fly being invited into the spider's parlor. "I had a pretty strong feeling about the way things might go if you went from door to door on your own," she readily admitted. The man, in her opinion, was much too good-looking for his own good.

They went on to knock on another two dozen doors by the time they decided to call it quits for the time being. At that point, they had knocked on a number of apartments on both sides of the residential development, moving farther and farther out as they went.

Most of the people they did find didn't recognize Carrie. Or, if they did, it was only vaguely from passing her by. No one had any information on a possible boyfriend.

Cody was disappointed to say the least.

"That's it?" he asked Skylar.

"Just for now," she answered. "We can pick up

where we left off tomorrow. Listen, why don't we grab some early dinner and then you can use the rest of the evening to go through your sister's things in her apartment? There's a possibility that you could find something helpful right off the bat. You might as well do that, because I'm pretty sure you're not going to get much sleep tonight—if any."

Cody looked at her, mildly surprised at the detective's insight.

Skylar could almost read his thoughts. "This is not my first rodeo, if you'll pardon the expression."

"I will if you will," he told her.

The grin she flashed at him was a broad one. "Consider it done," Skylar said.

Cody caught himself thinking that the detective really had a nice smile. It seemed to brighten the very room around her.

"When it comes to eating, do you have any particular preference in mind?" Skylar asked.

In response, Cody shrugged indifferently. "Just food," he replied.

"That gives me lots of leeway," she said. Then she smiled as a thought came to her. "And I think I have just the place for you."

"Some fast-food place nearby?" he guessed. He'd heard that California had a variety of fast-food places nestled all over. But, quite honestly, he really wasn't very hungry, Cody thought. If anything, he just needed to ingest a little something to keep him going.

"Not exactly."

"I'm not in the mood for a restaurant," he warned her. That was really the last place he wanted to go.

"That's good," Skylar answered, "because I'm not taking you to one."

"So where *are* you taking me?" he asked.

"Malone's," she answered.

That told him less than nothing. He'd never heard of the place. "What's Malone's?"

"Malone's is a bar owned by an ex-cop. He and some of his friends run it. And they serve really good food. I guarantee that going there will make you feel good. I can't explain it any better than that, but the food is excellent and the atmosphere there gives you hope," she told him.

"I wasn't planning on drinking myself into oblivion," Cody told her.

"That wasn't what I was suggesting," she said. "It's almost like a brotherhood at Malone's. They're all mostly cops that stop by there."

"I don't need a brotherhood," he stated.

"Well, we do have questions," she reminded him, "and who knows, they might have the right answers. Stranger things have happened. We don't have to stay very long. Just long enough for you to chew and swallow."

"Can't we just get something to go?" he asked her.

"We could," she allowed, agreeable. "But just do it my way this one time."

He frowned. She was making it sound as if they were going to be involved in some long-term relationship rather than just one that could be over in a matter of days.

He was tempted to ask just how long she expected this investigation to run, but decided he was too drained right now to get into the ramifications of that. So instead, he gave her a time limit.

"Ten minutes."

Because he was still attempting to come to terms with the fact that his sister had been killed, Skylar nodded, amenable to the terms he'd laid out for her.

She thought of the man in the back who prepared most of the food at Malone's. A long-time cop who was a widower, he was now retired. Working at Malone's was his long-term commitment.

"It might take him a little bit of time to get the meal ready," she told Cody, "but I'll do my best to have Dave hurry him along."

"'Him'?" Cody asked as she parked the Crown Victoria police vehicle across the street from Malone's. It was a Monday, but the parking lot was already full.

"Jacob," she told him. "Jacob usually prepares all the meals at Malone's. They'd have to strong-arm him to take a day off," she explained. "They're all good guys here." She sounded as if she was making a promise.

He wasn't looking to form a life-long friendship, or any sort of a friendship at all, he thought. All he wanted was to just grab something simple to fill his empty stomach. His stomach was making itself known right now, reminding him that even if he wasn't hungry, he needed to eat something to give him the energy to put one foot in front of the other.

At least until he could catch the lowlife that had killed his sister.

Besides, he'd discovered that it took less effort to agree with Skylar than it took to argue with her.

Resigned, Cody nodded his head.

Chapter 6

Malone's was fairly crowded, although there were still a few empty tables available in the rear of the bar where they could grab a seat. Cody noticed that several people called out a greeting to Skylar as they walked in.

She returned the greetings warmly.

This was obviously her hangout, Cody realized, though he had no interest in doing that. Still, he didn't want to interfere. He appreciated her efforts to help him find out what had happened to Carrie.

"Look," he told her, putting his hand on her shoulder to stop her, "if you want to stay here, I can grab a cab or an Uber and have it take me back to the police station so I can pick up my car," he offered. He had no intention of getting in her way.

Skylar looked at him in surprise. "You haven't eaten yet," she pointed out. "We're here so that you can get something to eat, remember? Speaking of which, what do you feel like having? A burger or something else?"

He was about to tell her that he was perfectly capable of ordering his own food, but since she probably knew what was good here and what was just passable, Cody decided to leave that choice up to her.

With a shrug, Cody said, "Whatever you pick out will be fine with me."

Skylar nodded good-naturedly. "A male who's not fussy. I've got to say that you're a breath of fresh air, Cody Cassidy," she told the deputy as she glanced toward the bar. "Wait here. I'll be right back."

Cody nodded, not bothering to comment one way or the other. Instead, he look a long look around at his surroundings. As far as bars went, Malone's wasn't all that different from the two bars he frequented back in Kiowa—except for a couple of minor things. Malone's was far better lit than the bars back home, plus there was no smoke lingering in the air. People in Malone's were talking and drinking, and a few of them were eating, but as he looked around the bar again, Cody didn't see a single person in the establishment who was smoking.

Technically, no one was supposed to be smoking back in Kiowa, either, but no one really took that to heart in the small town. Oh, there were a few diehards who did smoke; however, for the most part, the smokers could be found among the old-timers.

He had to admit that the idea of not taking in a lungful of smoke when he ate, especially since he was a nonsmoker, was a rather welcome change of pace from the bars in Kiowa.

Just then, Cody saw Skylar heading toward him. The detective was carrying a tray in her hands. On it were two plates plus a mug of ale and a glass that looked as if it had something in it that was fizzing.

Ginger ale? Cody caught himself wondering.

Rising from his seat, Cody took the tray from Skylar, then looked down at it. He thought she had said something about a burger, but there were no burgers on the tray. Had he misheard her?

She saw the quizzical look on his face. "I got you a hot roast beef sandwich on French bread," she told Cody. "This is actually a little faster to prepare than a hamburger. I also thought you might like to wash it down with a beer."

Setting the tray down, Cody saw that she had gotten a roast beef sandwich for herself as well. But that definitely wasn't a beer next to it.

He slanted a look back at Skylar, his eyes indicating the tall fizzing glass. "Is that what I think it is?"

"Depends on what you think it is," she answered, amusement in her blue eyes.

"Ginger ale." It was more of a question on his part than a statement. For all he knew, it was some fancy California drink.

"Then it is what you think it is," she told him, shifting her plate and the tall glass from the tray to the table. Tucking the tray to the side, she sat. "That roast beef sandwich tastes good even when it's cold, but it's even better if you eat it hot, which I highly recommend."

He obliged and took a bite, aware that Skylar was watching him chew. That made him feel somewhat self-conscious, until the taste had a chance to sink in. She was right, he thought. The sandwich really *was* good.

"Why isn't there some sort of game on in the background?" he asked her. There was a TV set mounted high up on the wall, but it was conspicuously dark.

"I think we're at the end of one season and not quite into another," she told Cody. "Besides, the people who came in are busy catching up with one another. Having a game going on right now would definitely interfere with talking. If nothing else, it would be distracting."

Things were definitely different in Malone's, he mused. "Where I come from, people go into a bar to *get* distracted," Cody told her.

"There are all sorts of ways to get distracted," Skylar assured the deputy. "A lot of times, the people are talking about the cases they're either working or have just solved. As a matter of fact, talking things out and saying them out loud helps the people in here put the pieces together."

Cody felt as if a light just went off in his head. "Is that why you brought me here?"

"I brought you here for the roast beef," she told him innocently, then cheerfully added, "Anything else is just gravy, if you don't mind the comparison."

Cody sincerely doubted that any of the officers or detectives who were here right now could give him any sort of insight into what had happened to his sister. However, being around Skylar and her positive attitude did give him the tiniest sliver of hope.

Still, Cody shrugged at her assessment. If he didn't buy into her words, he wouldn't wind up getting his hopes up. "If you say so."

"Hi, Sky." A tall, broad-shouldered, dark-haired man in jeans and a slightly rumpled, dark blue jacket made his way over and greeted the woman. He was holding a mug of partially completed ale as he quickly assessed the man with her. He nodded toward Cody. "Who's your friend?" he asked, quickly taking measure of the deputy.

"This is Deputy Cody Cassidy from Kiowa, New Mexico," she told her cousin. "Cody, this is Logan Cavanaugh, my uncle Sean's son. Sean heads up the Crime Scene Investigation Unit," she added, thinking it was just a matter of time before Cody met Sean.

Recognition crossed Logan's face. They had never met, but he knew of the deputy. "You're the one who came out here looking to find out what happened to his sister," Logan acknowledged. For the moment, he straddled the third chair at the table his cousin had commandeered. "I'm sorry to hear about your loss, Deputy. We're all keeping our ears open."

Considering that he had only been here for a little more than a day, Cody looked at the other man in complete surprise.

"Sounds like word here gets around really fast," he commented.

Logan ginned disarmingly as he shrugged. "You have no idea, Deputy," he said by way of confirmation. "Do you have anything to go on or any leads?"

"Even less than I thought I did when I got here," Cody confessed. He didn't like spinning his wheels like this, especially since it was all so personal to him.

Logan eyed his cousin. "Is that some sort of code?" he asked her, curious.

Skylar glanced at Cody, leaving the response to him—unless he indicated that he found it less awkward to have her answer her cousin.

In general, Cody was basically a private person. But when everything was said and done, this was not a private matter. Keeping a lid on things was not going to tell him who killed his twin, or why.

Taking a breath, he forged ahead. "Carrie and I were always close, to the point where we could end each other's sentences. We always knew what the other was thinking. But things changed when she came out to Aurora nine months ago. Her calls got less frequent, until they almost stopped coming altogether. And when I called her the last few times, the calls all went to voice mail first. She eventually did return them—until she didn't," he concluded.

"Was her moving to Aurora your sister's first time away from home?" Logan asked.

Cody felt he knew where this was going, but Skylar's cousin was wrong. "Yes, but that shouldn't have made a difference in communication. And if Carrie did meet someone, I would have been the first one she would have called to tell. She didn't."

Logan thought the information over. Coming from what could be thought of as a giant family, he did possess some insight into that situation.

"Maybe she was trying to hang on to her privacy," Logan suggested.

Cody shook his head, rejecting that theory. "Not Carrie."

Logan smiled. "Sisters can be funny that way," he told his cousin's new friend. "They're not always predictable," he all but guaranteed. "Trust me. I've got three of them, not to mention a parcel of female cousins—"

"And none of us have killed him yet," Skylar interjected, "which is pretty amazing all in itself."

Logan rose from the table, taking his all but empty beer mug with him. "And that's my cue to leave," he said with a good-natured nod toward Skylar. "I'll keep my ears open, Deputy. If I hear anything, I'll be sure to let you know," the detective promised. "Until then, I'll see you around."

Curious, Cody looked at the woman who was left at his table after her cousin walked off. "Just what did he mean by that? That he'd see me around?"

"Well," she explained, "we're a very close family. Our paths wind up crossing all the time. Plus, there're also the parties that Uncle Andrew throws practically all the time."

Cody looked at her, lost. "Excuse me, what?" he asked.

To enlighten him, Skylar backed up a few steps. "Uncle Andrew was the former chief of police in Aurora. He had to retire to take care of his five kids when his wife went missing—"

"Did he ever find her?" Cody asked, curious.

"Long story, but yes, he did. Uncle Andrew always had a gift for cooking, and he still likes getting the family together under any pretext he can come up with to cook for them—and the family likes being brought together. And eating, of course," she added with a wide grin.

"What does this have to do with me?" Cody asked.

"Anyone remotely connected to the police department—*any* police department," she stressed, looking at him pointedly, "Uncle Andrew considers them to be part of the family."

As far as Cody saw it, this just struck him as additional obstacles to get in the way of his investigation of his sister's killer and he said as much.

"I just want to find my sister's killer," he told her.

"And we will," Skylar promised with feeling. "This crowd takes things very seriously," she told him. "No matter how much they might seem like they're kidding around, it's just their way of knocking off steam. Every one of them prides himself—or herself—on being not just a decent cop, but a damn good cop."

Skylar had never meant anything more in her life.

He wasn't sure whether or not to believe her. After all, this was her family she was talking about. Would she say anything less than flattering about them?

He didn't know her well enough to hazard a guess about that.

In any case, he was way too mentally exhausted and drained to contest what she was saying at the moment.

"Good to know," Cody murmured noncommittally.

As they began to make good their escape, they wound up running into another branch of her family just coming in to grab a quick bite to eat.

After greeting Skylar, they asked to be introduced to her companion. They were all aware that it wasn't often that Skylar came into Malone's with a man who wasn't her partner or someone she *wasn't* related to.

That was when she remembered that she hadn't heard from Rio yet. Catching hold of Brennan, her late uncle Fergus's eldest son, she introduced him to Cody and asked him to handle the rest of the introductions to the deputy.

When Cody looked at her quizzically, she told him, as well as her cousins, "I need to call my partner to see how his wife is doing. I'll be right back," she promised all of them.

The only private place to make the call was the ladies' room.

Going in, she was happy to find herself alone. She knew that wouldn't last. Feeling guilty that she hadn't followed up until now, Skylar called her partner's cell phone.

After five rings, her call went to voice mail. She empathized with Cody, thinking how frustrating it must have been for him to keep calling and winding up being forced to listen to a prerecorded message before leaving a message that wasn't returned.

Skylar decided to try again before going through the routine. So she called again.

And again.

The fourth time around, she finally left a message.

"Rio, it's just me—Skylar," she added in case he didn't recognize her voice. "I hope you're just too busy to answer you phone and that Marsha is all right. Give me a call and let me know—any time. Doesn't matter if it's the middle of the night. *Call me*," she emphasized. "Meanwhile, I'm working with Cody Cassidy and trying to find out just what happened to his sister." She decided to let him know just where the investigation stood at this point. "Right now, it's just frustration all around. No one seems to know anything.

"Again, call me with any news," she requested just before she ended the call. With a deep sigh, she put her cell phone into her pocket.

Walking back into the bar, she half expected to have to go looking for Cody. The deputy struck her as someone who, if he got it into his head, would just take off.

Crossing her fingers, Skylar looked around, then paused by the bar to talk to the owner.

"That guy who came in with me," she said to Nathan. "Do you know if he's still here, or did he take off?"

Looking up from the counter he polished religiously several times an evening, the heavyset man smiled at her in response and then pointed toward the rear of the establishment.

Skylar turned around to see that Cody was talking to several members of her family. Unless she missed her guess, he looked rather comforted by the exchange he was engaged in.

Bless them for coming through, she thought, looking at her family fondly.

Chapter 7

"Everything okay with your partner's wife?" Duncan asked when he saw Skylar returning to the table that she had just recently vacated. At this point, Duncan and his brothers were sitting around it, talking to Cody.

Cody's back was to her, but he turned to face her and hear Skylar's answer to her cousin's question.

"I don't know," she replied honestly. "He's not picking up his phone."

"You could try calling the hospital and identify yourself, giving them the particulars of the accident," Bryce, another one of her cousins, suggested. "Ask if Rio's wife has been admitted or sent home."

She had already thought of that just now. "I'll do that as soon as I take Cody here back to the police station so he can pick up his car." Skylar looked at the deputy. "Are you ready to go?"

Cody rose to his feet. "Yeah."

"I can take him there, Sky," Duncan volunteered.

She smiled at her cousin. "Thank you, but I always finish what I start. Or have you forgotten that?"

Duncan exchanged looks with a couple of his brothers, rolling his eyes as he put his hand over his heart.

"Heaven forbid," he told her. Duncan's attention turned to Cody. "Nice meeting you, Cody, but very sorry about the circumstances behind your visit to our fair city," he told the deputy.

"Don't worry, we'll get him," Brennan promised, shaking Cody's hand.

We'll get him.

The words echoed in Cody's head. Skylar's cousins made it sound like it was a group project, as if they were all involved in this, Cody couldn't help thinking. Were these people for real?

He believed in being dedicated and doing his job, but as far as he knew, these detectives hadn't been assigned to the case. Why did they make it sound as if they were all involved in finding his sister's killer?

He didn't get it.

On his way out, he stopped at the bar, took out his wallet and said to Dave, "I'd like to settle my tab. Our tab," he corrected himself, glancing at Skylar. Since she had brought him here, he thought it only right that he cover her meal.

Dave waved away Cody's wallet. "It's already been settled," he told.

Cody took that to mean that Skylar had paid the bill. "I can pay my own bills," he told her, annoyed.

"I'm sure you can," she answered. "But don't look at me. I didn't pay the tab. Right, Dave?" she asked the bar's owner.

"Right," the former police officer answered. "And before you ask, the person who did pay your tab wishes to remain anonymous. As a good business-man, I have to respect their wishes." Inclining his head, Dave told the duo, "Have a nice night—and don't forget to come back." His words followed them to the front door.

Cody waited until he had gotten in on the passen-ger side of the detective's car and she had started up the engine before he asked, "Just when did you get a chance to pay the tab?"

"I didn't," she replied, looking at him innocently.

"Okay, then who did?" he asked.

"I guess that's just going to be one of those mys-teries of life that will remain permanently unan-swered," she told him, guiding the vehicle out of the parking lot.

Cody frowned. "You mean to tell me that this is a regular thing?"

"No," she answered, doing a U-turn and pulling onto the road. "It's a once-in-a-while thing," she an-swered, correcting the deputy. "Just accept it as a good deed done by a good person. Most likely, it was someone in my family and they had to pay my bill as well because, otherwise, it would look too suspicious. Consider it as someone saying 'welcome to Aurora.'"

That still didn't sit well with him. He had his pride. "I can pay my own bills."

"So you said. No one said you couldn't," she pointed out. "Just let it go, Cody. Lord knows that you have enough on your mind right now."

That he did, he conceded, struggling to keep the grief from eating him up alive. And then, almost immediately after that thought, he looked at it from Skylar's point of view.

"I'm sorry," he apologized. "I didn't mean to sound as if I was reading you the riot act just now."

Approaching a red light, Skylar glanced in Cody's direction. "Don't worry about it. I know how I'd feel in your place," she told him. "Speaking of which, how are you holding up?"

He was surprised by the question. It was almost too personal, too understanding. "One foot in front of the other," he told her. "Just keeping one foot in front of the other."

Skylar bobbed her head at the admission. "Best way to handle it," she assured him. The next moment, she pulled up into the station parking lot and drove toward where Cody had parked his vehicle.

"Well, there's your car," she said, waving at it. And then she made a quick decision. "Look, why don't I follow you to your sister's apartment?" she suggested.

Did she think that he forgot where the apartment

complex was located? Cody frowned. "I know where it is."

"I didn't mean to suggest that you didn't. But a lot of unfamiliar things look and seem different at nighttime than they do in daylight. I just think it might help you if you have someone lead the way to the complex, get you settled in, that sort of thing."

She saw his frown intensifying and knew what that had to mean. "I just think you might feel better that way. And just so you know," she added, "I'm not planning on staying and hovering. I wouldn't want it to be any different than if you were my brother, trying to solve my murder and someone offered you their help," she informed him.

He looked at her, totally surprised by the sentiment she'd just expressed. "You really mean that, don't you?"

"Yes," she answered very simply. "I really do. And I'm not doing this for you. I'm doing this for your sister," she told him, adding with conviction, "She would want me to."

"You never met my sister—did you?" he felt compelled to ask.

"No, I didn't," she answered. "But I have brothers, and we're all close, although I would probably have to put them in an inflexible headlock before they'd publicly admit to that," Skylar told him.

She had pulled up beside his vehicle, waiting for him to tell her whether he was going to take her up on her offer or not.

Cody thought about it for a long moment, then

got out of her car. "All right," he told her, opening his car door. "If it makes you happy, you can follow me to Carrie's apartment."

That was undoubtedly a comment on what he took to be her pushiness, Skylar thought. But that was okay. She had meant what she'd said. That she was doing this for his sister—because if something had happened to her, she would want to have someone helping her brothers, as well as her sisters, deal with the situation as well as cope with it.

It was the best way she could attempt to explain the situation—and her reaction to it—to Cody.

There was very little traffic from the police station to the development where Carrie Cassidy had lived the last nine months of her life. Following him, Skylar waited until Cody parked his car in the space assigned to Carrie's apartment.

Once he did, she went on to park the Crown Victoria in guest parking.

Getting out, she locked her car and quickly hurried over to Cody.

He stood there, waiting for her beside his vehicle. "Afraid I'd try to ditch you?" he asked her, curious.

"I just didn't want to keep you waiting."

"Are you always this thoughtful?"

"Pretty much," she answered, humor playing along the corners of her mouth.

The truth of it was, Skylar didn't want him walking into the apartment by himself for the first time at night. She was fairly confident that the loneliness that would register might be too much for him to bear.

She knew she was crediting him with her own thoughts and feelings, but she couldn't really help that.

Cody unlocked the door and Skylar went in first, turning on lights as she made her way through the apartment. Almost all of the lights were on when she was finished.

"Are you afraid of the dark?" he asked her, slightly amused. "Or are you just in league with the electric company?"

"Neither," she answered. "But with the lights on, the apartment just looks warmer and more welcoming."

That struck him as an odd thing to say. And then he realized why she had said that.

"Having the lights on doesn't change anything," Cody told her. His sister was still gone.

"No," Skylar agreed. "But it might make it a little easier to put up with."

He wanted to say that nothing would make it easier to put up with, but he knew that the detective's heart was in the right place, so he didn't want to give her a hard time. In her own way, she was just attempting to make it more bearable for him. "I'll be all right," Cody told her.

She wasn't all that sure that he would be right now. "I can stay with you for a while," she offered.

"There is no need to do that," Cody informed her.

"I know," she replied simply. "Maybe I just want to."

He caught himself wondering if she was afraid

that he might do something drastic. "I don't want to keep you up," he told her. "Go home and get some sleep."

"All right," she agreed. The last thing she wanted was to appear to be throwing herself at him, or burrowing her way into his life. "I'll be back first thing tomorrow morning."

"Just what do you consider 'first thing'?" he asked.

"Six a.m. Seven a.m.," she declared. "Whatever you're comfortable with."

What he was comfortable with would be working this case on his own, but Aurora wasn't exactly his home territory, so he wasn't able to dictate terms.

"You pick," she told him.

She stared at him for a long moment. "All right, I'll be back here tomorrow morning at seven," she announced.

He looked at her, surprised. "Seven?" he questioned. "You don't want to sleep in?"

"I never sleep in," she informed him. "For the most part, I've always felt that sleep is a waste of time."

"Carrie would have gotten a real big kick out of you," Cody said with a slight laugh.

"Because she agreed with my philosophy, or because she didn't?" Skylar asked.

A fond look came over his face as he thought about his twin. "Carrie usually went ninety miles an hour, working really, really hard, so whenever she had a chance to catch up on her sleep, she did."

"She sounds like she was a really great person to know," Skylar told him.

A fond, wistful expression crossed his face. "She was."

Skylar leaned forward and squeezed his hand. "We'll get whoever is responsible for this, Cody. I promise you we will."

He studied her for a very long moment. "You can't make that promise," he asserted. "It's not in your power to make it."

"Oh, yes, I can," she proclaimed.

She was utterly serious, he thought.

Cody wanted to believe her, wanted to believe that she meant this promise that she had just made him, despite the fact that there was no way in the world she could actually keep it.

Cody had no idea what had possessed him, what had made him lean forward, causing his space to invade hers. But one moment he was discounting her words, despite the fact that he felt this overwhelming desperate need to take those words to heart. The next moment, his lips found hers.

He had absolutely no idea how that had happened, or even why. The closest thing he could ascribe it to was that he *needed* to believe her, needed to believe that his sister—the person he had shared every moment with for all these years—couldn't just slip away like that, out of his life, without his at least avenging her.

Cody slipped his arms around Skylar, pulling her to him. Kissing her as if there wasn't going to be a tomorrow. Because if this detective wasn't able to help him solve the mystery of Carrie's death, then there would *be* no tomorrow. Not for him.

Abruptly, Cody pulled away, his lips leaving hers as he dropped his hands to his sides. Clearing his throat, he looked at her as if he hadn't seen her before.

"I'm sorry," he told Skylar uncomfortably.

"No reason to apologize." She smiled at Cody. "Just one soul reaching out to another, looking for some sort of comfort..." Skylar hesitated. "I'll see myself out," she told him as she walked over to the front door. "And I'll be here at seven—unless another time suits you better?" She offered to make the change one last time.

"Seven will be fine," he answered, his eyes meeting hers. Most likely, he wouldn't get any sleep anyway, Cody thought.

"Seven it is," Skylar replied.

She congratulated herself on making it out the garden apartment door without a mishap.

Her legs felt extremely wobbly.

Chapter 8

By a little past six the next morning, Skylar was not only up and dressed, she had to force herself to wait until it was at least seven thirty.

While she was fairly convinced that Cody had undoubtedly had trouble falling asleep, if he had even managed to drop off at what was probably a really late hour, she didn't want to risk waking him if he *had* accumulated an hour or so of sleep.

To while away the time—and because she believed in being productive—she made herself a quick breakfast to go, packed another one for the deputy, and went on to prepare coffee for both of them. She poured some milk into a separate container, took a few packets of sugar and tossed in a handful of napkins as well.

Once Skylar had everything she thought she might need, she closed the containers and flipped the locks.

She was out the door well before seven, hoping that Cody hadn't jumped the gun and left before she'd even had a chance to get to his garden apartment.

Settling in behind the wheel of her Crown Victoria, she started up the vehicle. It occurred to her that she was taking an awful lot for granted when it came to Cody Cassidy. After all, how much did she really know about the man? At this point, she was just taking his word for things.

Skylar supposed that she could run a background check on the deputy. But considering the size of the Kiowa police department, she was trusting that the people in Cody's station would volunteer the information she needed without any prejudice.

That might not turn out to be the case.

But then, she came from a family that had taught her to look for the best in people rather than to suspect the worst. So, unless she was shown otherwise, she was going to just assume that Cody was on the straight and narrow.

Besides, she thought with a smile, a man who could make the world go away by kissing her like that definitely couldn't be all that bad.

"Okay, Sky, get your mind back on your work," she lectured herself, pulling into the development where the deputy was currently staying.

She wondered if Cody had gotten any sleep at all. She certainly hoped so. He would have to be clear-headed to attempt to make any sense of the information he was probably going to have to sort through—and that was only if he wound up getting lucky.

Parking proved to be a challenge inasmuch as all the available spaces in guest parking appeared to be taken at first.

There had to have been a great many overnight guests last night, Skylar mused.

She had almost circled the immediate area before she spotted an empty space. Backing up, she reversed toward the spot until she managed to slip into it.

Getting out, she assessed her surroundings. The parking space was some distance away from the garden apartment. But a little exercise, she reasoned, never hurt. She usually ran a couple of miles before breakfast in the morning, but today had been different.

In Cody's place, she would have been anxious to get back to the "hunt." He wasn't going to feel whole again until he found the man who had done this to his sister.

Taking the breakfast she had prepared for them, Skylar walked up to the apartment door. She was about to ring the bell when the door unexpectedly swung open and Cody suddenly exited.

He hadn't anticipated her being right there and they all but collided.

Startled, Skylar took a couple of steps back. Collecting herself, she laughed at his making such an unexpected appearance. "That's some radar you have," she told him.

For a second, the detective had managed to lose him. But then he realized what she was saying. She seemed to think that he'd been anticipating her on his doorstep.

"That's not radar," Cody told her. "I was just getting an early start this morning."

"Without me?" she questioned as she made her way into the apartment.

"I'm a grown man," he stated. "I made it from Kiowa to Aurora. I can certainly handle smaller distances. Besides, the car's old, but it does come with a GPS." He followed her into the small kitchen. She was making herself at home, he noted. "And, when all else fails," Cody went on, "there're always maps to use. I do have one in the car," he told her.

She didn't know if he was being serious, or just humoring her. In either case, she decided to just ignore the incident and especially the sarcasm that came with it. She thought it was safer that way than to risk a flare-up first thing in the morning.

Cody suddenly paused and sniffed the air around Skylar. "You brought coffee," he declared. It was hardly a guess.

"And breakfast," she added. "I thought you might want some. I don't know if you're the type who eats first thing in the morning, but I decided to take a chance and bring you some, just in case."

He watched her unpack. It smelled even more tempting once she took out the individually wrapped packages. He looked over the two bags she had placed on the counter.

"There's no label on the packages," Cody noted.

"That's because I don't have a labeler," she told him.

His forehead wrinkled as he took the information in. "This didn't come from a fast-food place?" he questioned. He'd assumed that she would have just picked up something at a drive-thru before getting here.

"Not unless you consider my kitchen to be a fast-food place," she told him.

She picked up the two bags and placed them on the small kitchen table. She then proceeded to look through the drawers for the utensils and found them on her second try.

Taking out two forks for the breakfast muffins and two spoons for the coffee containers, she set the utensils on the table. Turning, she opened the overhead cabinets. Rummaging through the small spaces, she didn't locate any regular plates.

Instead, there were just paper ones, some large, some small. There were also a couple of plastic plates next to them as well.

"Didn't your sister have any regular plates?" Skylar asked. From what Cody had mentioned, his sister had lived here for around nine months. Not having any plates in that time seemed rather odd to her.

Cody glanced into the cabinet, even though he already knew the answer. "I don't think so," he replied. "Carrie never liked washing dishes." Anticipating her next question, Cody explained, "She kept the knives, forks and spoons because they were a housewarming gift from our father, but I'm fairly sure that she would have rather used plastic utensils."

Cody went on. "Just before she moved out here, I was all set to buy her a set of dinnerware, but she told me to save my money," he recalled. "So I wound up buying her a bunch of sheets and towels instead."

Skylar took all this in, nodding her head. "Your sister was a very unique young woman," she told Cody.

At this point, the detective was just preaching to the choir. "That she was," Cody agreed. There was more than a touch of wistfulness in his voice.

Skylar placed the breakfast sandwiches she had prepared earlier in her apartment onto the paper plates she had taken down from the cabinets, then moved those plates to the table settings, facing one another.

She saw Cody looking skeptically at the offerings.

"No offense, Skylar," he told her, "but I'm not all that hungry."

"Understood," she answered. "But you do need to keep up your strength and consuming this little bit of food will provide at least some of that for you." She saw the stubborn look that entered his eyes. "Let me put it to you this way—if you don't eat, you're not going to go anywhere."

Cody had never liked being ordered around. He dug in his heels. "And who is going to stop me?"

Skylar didn't hesitate for a single moment. "I am."

Which caused Cody to utter the typical challenge. "You and what army?"

Skylar smiled up at him, her eyes meeting his. "Just me."

The woman meant that, he realized. He could practically hear those same words coming from Carrie. The pretty, young detective really did remind him of his sister.

Cody sighed. He was not about to back off from the challenge he had uttered, but for the moment, he decided just to go along with her opposition.

"All right," he conceded, pulling the plate closer to him, "if it makes you happy, I'll eat."

Skylar flashed him a wide, good-natured smile. "It makes me very happy—and deep down, I suspect that consuming the breakfast I made will make you feel very happy, too."

The breakfast she had prepared for each of them was a fried egg, with bacon strips, covered in melted cheese and encased in a toasted muffin. And while the offering wasn't exactly hot, transported the way it had been in a plastic container, it was still somewhat warm, which was all she'd been hoping for.

Watching Cody pick up the muffin and sink his teeth into it, she was more than a little gratified when she saw the startled smile grace his lips.

"So, do you like it?" she asked, rather certain what the deputy's answer was going to be.

"I do," he responded, surprised as he looked at the muffin, egg, cheese and bacon combination. He raised his eyes to hers. "And you made this?"

"Yes. Why does that surprise you?" she asked. "You told me that your sister cooked." Why would he think that she couldn't?

"Yes, but Carrie had to—from a very young age," he told her. "My mother was sick for a number of years, so Carrie just took over all the chores whenever she could. And whenever she couldn't, my father and I would pitch in, although, admittedly, our combined effort didn't match Carrie's."

"In my family, we all took turns doing chores. And I mean *all*—" she emphasized the word "—of us."

"I'm impressed."

And he looked it, too, Skylar thought.

"Nothing to be impressed about. That's just what being part of a family is," Skylar told him, her eyes crinkling just a little as she smiled at him. "You don't have a corner on that particular market."

He looked down at the paper plate before him and was stunned to see that he had managed to finish his breakfast without even realizing it.

Wiping his mouth and fingers with the napkin Skylar had set out, he pronounced, "This was really good."

"I'm glad you approve," she told Cody, tongue-in-cheek. Rising, she picked up the utensils, put them into the sink, then went on to throw out the paper plates. "Well, this certainly made cleanup a lot easier. Maybe your sister was on to something."

He had to admit that he did get a kick out of Skylar's statement. "She did have a way about her," he agreed. Glancing at his watch, he said, "And having breakfast here did eat up a little bit more time."

"Looks like it was a win-win situation," Skylar replied. And then she looked at Cody. "Are you ready to go?"

"More than ready," he told her. "Do you want to use my car—or yours?"

"We'll drive to the police station separately," she said assertively, "so you're not stranded if I get called away. But for the most part we'll use mine. After all, this is official police business and using my vehicle makes it easier to maintain that this is official," she told Cody.

"All right," he agreed as he stepped out of the apartment and looked toward the closest guest parking area. "Where is your car?" he asked.

Skylar pointed off into the distance. Since she had arrived and had parked the Crown Victoria, several spaces, much closer than the one she had used, had opened up.

"It's right there," she told him.

"That's a pretty long walk from the apartment," he commented.

She merely smiled. "Helps me keep my weight down," she answered. She hadn't mentioned that there hadn't been any opened spaces earlier. He walked with her.

"What weight?" Cody asked seriously.

"See?" she responded cheerfully. "It's working already."

When they reached her vehicle, Skylar paused

next to the driver's side and told the deputy, "I'm going to swing by the lieutenant's office to give him an update."

Had he missed something? Cody wondered. "There isn't any update," he noted.

"That, too, is an update in itself," she pointed out. She saw the impatient look creasing the deputy's forehead. "You know as well as I do that these things take time. They only get solved in a set amount of time in the movies and on television programs. Everything else is documented to death," she told him.

Cody blew out a breath. "Yes, I know that," he responded. "But that doesn't make waiting any easier."

Skylar nodded, sympathizing with him completely.

In addition, she had already thought of what their next move was going to be once they left the police station. "Do you know where your sister worked before she left her job?"

"She was a substitute teacher at a local high school," he answered, holding the driver's door for her as she got in.

"Do you know which local high school?" she asked.

"I do. Venado," he recalled.

"Then that'll be our next stop after I talk to the lieutenant," she told him.

"By the way, did you ever wind up reaching your partner?" he queried. "Last night, your call kept going to voice mail."

She was surprised, with all that the deputy had

on his mind, that Cody remembered her messages hadn't reached Rio yesterday.

"Yes, I did finally reach him. His wife had to have emergency surgery, but from all indications, she seemed to have come through it well. When I spoke to him, he said she was in a medically induced coma. He promised to keep me informed of her condition."

"When did you speak to him?" he asked.

"A little after one this morning," she answered.

He looked at her in wonder. "You don't seem exhausted. You should be more tired than I am," Cody told her.

Skylar smiled and pulled out her keys. "I didn't tell you, did I?"

She was losing him again. "Tell me what?"

"I run on batteries." She started her engine. "Get your car, Cassidy," she urged.

She didn't have to tell him twice.

Chapter 9

Within twenty-five minutes, after touching base with Lieutenant Anderson and letting the man know that her partner, Rio, was taking some personal time to be at his wife's hospital bedside, Skylar and Cody were back in her car.

"You said that Carrie previously worked as a substitute teacher before she decided to end her employment. Do you know exactly when she terminated her contract and why?"

He thought for a moment, going back to one of the last conversations he'd had with his sister. He really didn't know why red flags hadn't gone up at the time.

"She said she was looking for a better work environment," he answered. He should have pressed

Carrie about that, Cody realized. "That was about a little more than almost two months ago."

"That's just about the time when your sister stopped answering your phone calls," Skylar said. "You didn't think that was odd?"

In hindsight, he did, and he really regretted that he hadn't acted on that feeling. All he'd had at the time was the reason he had assumed he couldn't reach her. "I just thought she was busy trying to get started in this 'new' career of hers."

That sounded rather suspect to Skylar. "Did she happen to share what this new career was?" she asked.

Cody called himself seven kinds of a fool as he shrugged his shoulders. "She said it was going to be a surprise." The deputy sighed and stared straight ahead. "A surprise," he repeated, mocking himself. "How could I have been such a fool?"

"Because you're not clairvoyant," she told him, trying to get him to lighten up on himself. "Because you wanted to give Carrie her space, like a good brother."

"I wasn't just her brother, I was her *twin*," he decreed, angry with the way he had dropped the ball. "What that means is that I should have *known*, should have *sensed,* that there was something wrong." Upset, Cody took himself to task. "But I didn't."

The traffic light at the intersection turned red and she stopped, glancing at Cody. "I don't profess to begin to understand what that connection between you and your twin was like at bottom. I just have a lot of siblings. What I do know is that you're not going to be able to avenge what happened to Carrie by beating yourself up about it. That kind of attitude won't do you *or* your twin sister any good."

Cody frowned. He didn't like being lectured to, especially when he couldn't really argue with what she was saying.

Staring straight ahead, he all but grudgingly growled at her. "You're right."

"Why do I get the feeling that you just put a curse on me?" Skylar asked, trying her best to improve the mood just the least tiny bit.

"If I was going to put a curse on anyone," Cody responded, his voice sounding dejected, "it would be on me." What kind of a law enforcement officer did that make him? Cody upbraided himself.

"That would just be a huge waste of time," she replied in all seriousness. "Let's just focus on getting all the information we can so that we can bring whoever did this to justice. That means putting all the pieces together, no matter how fragmented they seem to be right now," she pointed out. Pausing at another red light, she looked at Cody, her eyes all but penetrating into him. "All right?" she asked.

He blew out a breath, trying to separate himself from the hopeless feeling that was suddenly threatening to swallow him whole.

"All right." He all but bit off the words. Then, after a moment's pause, Cody apologized. "I'm sorry. I'm usually a hell of a lot better at my job than this."

"I'm sure you are. This isn't exactly a standard

situation for you. You're allowed to be a little rattled. Or a lot rattled," she amended, thinking the situation over and feeling for the man. "Since this involves your sister, it makes a huge difference."

It took Skylar a second to realize that they had arrived at their destination. She pulled into the lot in front of the entrance to the high school, though it took her a little time to find a parking space that didn't have a name posted in front of it.

As he got out, Cody looked in awe at all the cars that were parked in the lot. "Just how many teachers are there working here?"

She really had no idea, Skylar realized. "The usual number, I suppose. Why?" she asked as she led the way to the concrete stairs and then climbed them.

Cody glanced over his shoulder and assessed the vehicles. "Just seems like an awful lot of cars to me."

She knew what he had to be thinking. "Those cars don't belong to the teachers," Skylar told him. "They belong to the students." She knew that from experience. Some things didn't change. "The teachers park their vehicles in the parking lot located on the other side of the school."

Cody was surprised by what the detective said. He looked around the lot again. "Their parents must really be doing well," he marveled.

"To a degree, yes," Skylar agreed. "But I think that you'd be surprised to learn that a lot of the students who go here have after-school jobs and are putting that money toward paying off their cars. The kids today," she told him, "aren't all that different from a generation or two ago. That's not to say that they're all saints, either. They're just the usual mixture of good and bad."

Skylar led the way toward the outdoor stairway, which in turn brought them to the wide, squat, sprawling school building.

Cody realized that he was just following her blindly. "Do you know where you're going?" he asked, curious.

"Of course I do. The registrar's office," she answered. "I used to go to this school. Things haven't changed all that much in that time."

Cody had just assumed that she and her siblings hadn't attended public school. "You didn't attend private school?" he asked.

She turned to look at him as if the question he had just asked was nothing short of inane.

"You're kidding, right? The Cavanaughs are just about as down to earth as you can get," she told him. "Besides, the public school system in Aurora is exceptionally good. There's absolutely no need for private schools—or tutors," she added in case he wasn't convinced.

Approaching the registrar's office, Skylar politely knocked on the door, then opened it.

Flashing her credentials at the startled-looking assistant principal, who was sitting at the desk facing the door, Skylar said, "Excuse me. I'm Detective Cavanaugh with the APD and this is Deputy Cassidy from Kiowa, New Mexico. We would like to speak to the person in charge."

The woman, Ellen Hanks, nodded at the request. "That would be Principal Brad Larson, but he is out sick. I'm the assistant principal. May I ask what this is all about?"

"One of his former substitute teachers." By the look on the assistant principal's face, it was obvious the woman was waiting for a name. Skylar gave her one. "Carrie Cassidy."

There was no other way to say this, Skylar thought, but to say it outright. Avoiding Cody's eyes, she told the woman, "Ms. Cassidy was found floating in the lake several days ago."

Ellen Hanks immediately looked horror-stricken. "Are you sure it was Carrie?" she asked Skylar.

But it was Cody who answered. "We're sure," he said grimly.

The assistant principal took a closer look at the young man standing before her. "Are you by any chance related to Carrie?"

"Yes, I am," he admitted. "She was my sister."

The woman stood and circled her desk, coming out in front of it as if that made her sentiment somehow clearer.

"I am very sorry to hear that. Your sister only worked here for a short while, but everyone liked her. She was a very sweet, outgoing young woman. The students all responded to her," she informed them, predominantly Cody.

Skylar nodded. "Was she friends with anyone in particular? Someone we could talk to? We're trying to find out if she was seeing someone."

"You could talk to Nancy Nelson," the assistant principal recommended. "She and your sister used to have lunch together on Fridays. Like I said, Carrie got along with everyone, but she seemed closer to Nancy Nelson than to anyone else."

"Is Nancy Nelson here?" Cody asked, trying to move this along.

"Actually, she called in sick today—and yesterday, too, now that I think of it," the woman added.

"Do you have an address where we could reach this woman?" Skylar asked.

Ellen Hanks looked rather uncertain about the question. "We don't generally release addresses. This is highly unusual," the woman told them.

"So is murder," Skylar answered darkly.

"Murder?" the assistant echoed, clearly startled. "You think that Carrie Cassidy was murdered?"

"According to our medical examiner, that is a very real possibility," Skylar answered.

Ellen Hanks moved to sit in her desk chair, faced her computer and typed in the teacher's name. "As far as I know, this is Nancy Nelson's current address. I know she was looking for a bigger place to stay, but I don't think that she found it yet. She certainly didn't update her address for our records."

Writing the address down, the woman handed it to the detective.

Skylar looked the address over. The location wasn't far from where they currently were. "Thank you for this," she said, holding up the address the woman had handed her. "Was there anyone else Carrie Cassidy was close to here?" Skylar asked.

"Like I told you, Carrie got along with everyone," the assistant principal said. "Students and staff," she affirmed. "But I would say that Nancy is your best bet."

About to leave, Skylar looked down at the address again. Something else occurred to her. "Would you happen to know if Carrie was seeing anyone?"

Ellen Hanks looked torn, not to mention a little uncertain about releasing the information. "That would be prying," she answered.

"I'd see it as taking an active interest in the teaching staff," Skylar replied, putting a different spin on it.

"Well, now that you mention it, she did have a different glow about her just before she handed in her notice, but I really can't tell you any more than that with any sort of certainty," the woman confessed.

Skylar nodded. It had been a long shot, but she felt she had to try. "Well, thank you for Ms. Nelson's address," she told the woman.

"Don't mention it." The assistant principal's lips lifted in a quick, spasmodic smile. "Good luck," she called after the departing duo.

"If we don't get anywhere with this Nancy Nelson," Skylar told Cody as she drove toward the address that Ellen Hanks had given them, "we'll come back and see if we can interview the other teachers as well as the substitute teachers and question them. Someone has to know something about your sister's life."

"I was closer to her than anyone," Cody reminded her. "If she didn't tell me anything..." His voice trailed off.

She knew where he was going with this and she had an answer. "Sometimes it's easier to talk to a stranger than it is to talk to family or even close friends."

He glared at her as if she had sprouted another head.

"Trust me. If something was going on in her life and she just wanted to unload, a stranger is easier to talk to than someone who might be close to your sister," she told Cody.

He shook his head. He had always kept his own counsel rather than share things. "You women are a very confusing sex," he muttered.

She laughed. "Funny, that's what I always say about men," she joked. "I guess that's what keeps things interesting between the sexes."

Cody sighed, shaking his head. "If you say so."

Carrie's friend Nancy Nelson lived in the city next to Aurora, but it didn't take very long to get there. What did take long was getting her to answer the door.

It took three tries ringing the woman's doorbell before Nancy Nelson finally came to the front door. She appeared utterly miserable, like someone who was in the middle of nursing either the flu or an incredibly bad cold.

Watery eyes stared blankly at the people on her doorstep. The teacher wouldn't have opened the door

at all if Skylar hadn't held up her badge and identification for review.

"Is something wrong, Detective Cavanaugh?" the
teacher asked, punctuating her question with a deep
cough that all but vibrated throughout her chest.

"We're really sorry to bother you, Ms. Nelson,
but we need to ask you a few questions about Carrie Cassidy," Skylar told her.

Watery eyes flicked from the detective to the
good-looking man standing next to her. A man who
looked a great deal like her friend.

Nancy sneezed before taking a step back, out of
the doorway.

"Sure. I don't know if I'll be much help since I
haven't seen her for a couple of weeks. We were supposed to get together last week, but Carrie was a no-
show." There was curiosity in her eyes. "Is something
wrong?" the woman asked, punctuating her question
with another sneeze.

Rather than answer, Cody suggested, "Why don't
we go inside?"

Carrie's friend didn't like the sound of that, but
she led the way into the apartment.

Two deep coughs resonated, marking Nancy's
path back into her apartment.

Chapter 10

Looking at the two people through progressively more watery eyes, Nancy gestured toward the sofa in the small living room. "Why don't you sit down?" the woman suggested as she struggled to suppress yet another sneeze.

"I think that you need to sit down more than we do," Cody observed, having her walk in front of them.

Taking in a shaky breath, Nancy nodded wearily. "No argument. This cold is really wearing me out." She made her way over to the sofa and lowered herself onto it on shaky legs. "But you have me worried. Did something happen to Carrie?"

"What makes you ask that?" Cody asked. He couldn't help wondering if this woman had had something to do with his twin's demise.

Nancy shrugged helplessly. "Carrie was always very good about answering her phone, or at least returning her calls. But this time, even though I left her a message and asked why she hadn't turned up for lunch the way we'd arranged, I haven't heard word one from her. I thought maybe she was embarrassed because she was having a little trouble finding another job or..." Her voice trailed off like someone who suddenly felt as if she had said too much.

But Skylar wasn't about to let the matter drop. "Or?" she asked, trying to encourage Carrie's friend to continue. "Or what?"

Nancy sighed. She had started this, she might as well follow it to the end. "I thought she might be arguing with her boyfriend. The last time I talked to her, they'd had a few flare-ups," the young woman confided, lowering her voice even though there was no one around to overhear the exchange except for the three of them.

Cody immediately pounced on the information. "Did you ever meet him?"

"Once," Nancy admitted, then thought about her answer. "He came to pick her up at school about two months ago."

"Do you remember what his name was, or anything about what he looked like?" Skylar asked. She was trying to put together some sort of a picture of the man as well as to get a handle on the sort of relationship they shared.

Nancy nodded. The gesture seemed to hurt her head. "She introduced him as Brent Masterson and at the time I remember thinking that he seemed exceedingly charismatic—not to mention really, really handsome. I do remember that Carrie fell for him right from the beginning," the teacher admitted. "Hard."

About to say something further, the woman had to pause to blow her nose and then dab at her eyes, which had become watery again.

"Would you happen to know what he does for a living?" Skylar asked Carrie's friend conversationally, trying not to sound as if she were pressing her for more information.

Nancy shook her head. "Carrie never actually told me what he did, but I got the impression that it had something to do with the school. Maybe he was some sort of independent contractor," the teacher guessed with a shrug. "I really don't know that much about the man for sure," she told the two people in her living room. And then she added, with a pleased, triumphant smile, "I did sneak a picture of the two of them together."

Cody immediately became alert, exchanging looks with Skylar. "Do you happen to have that picture where you could get your hands on it?" the deputy asked.

The teacher thought for a minute, then nodded. "Give me a minute," Nancy told him. She rose with effort and made her way over to her closet. Her shoulder bag was hanging on a hook.

She fetched it and brought it back over to the sofa. Sitting, she opened the bag and took out her cell phone. Concentrating, the woman proceeded to flip through the photographs that were on it.

"There," she declared elatedly, holding up her phone for them to see. "It's a little blurry," she admitted, explaining the reason why. "I had to do it on the sly. Brent didn't like having his picture taken," she told the pair on her sofa. "Although I don't see why. He's the best-looking man I've seen in a long time—present company excluded, of course." The teacher smiled, looking at her friend's brother.

Red flags had immediately gone up in Skylar's head. She could only see two reasons for Carrie's significant other not liking having photographs taken of himself. He was either exceedingly shy—which hardly seemed likely to her way of thinking—or he was exceptionally leery of leaving behind a trail that would aid people in identifying him.

"I'd really appreciate getting a copy of that," she told the woman. "Let me give you my cell phone number and, if it's not too much trouble, you can send that photo to my phone. That's the only photograph you have, right?" she asked as an afterthought.

Nancy's laugh was half-hearted. "I'm lucky to have gotten that one," she told Skylar. "I don't mind telling you that when I was taking it, my heart almost stopped. Brent turned his head at the very last moment and almost caught me at it. That's why the photo is as blurry as it is," she explained. "He really didn't like having his picture taken."

"You did good." Skylar praised the woman. She

recited her cell number to Nancy and then waited for the successful transfer.

Her phone dinged, alerting her of the transfer, and she looked at the screen. "Not bad," Skylar commented, pleased. She held up her phone for Cody's benefit. "I think we've got enough for Valri to work with," she told him. Closing her phone, she tucked it into her back pocket and looked at the woman they had been talking to. "You've been a great help, Ms. Nelson." She rose to her feet.

Cody immediately stood as well.

"I think we should let you rest," she told Nancy, who chose that moment to sneeze again. "Bless you," Skylar said. Walking to the front door, she turned to look at the teacher. "If we have any other questions, we'll be in touch."

"Will you let me know how this winds up going?" Nancy asked, then added, "I really hope that Brent isn't responsible for anything that happened to her. He seemed like a really nice guy and, in my opinion, Carrie was crazy about him, at least in the beginning."

Cody focused on her words. "Oh?"

"Well, I wasn't there for the end of it," Nancy explained, "so I have no way of knowing if things went sour."

Skylar took the woman's words into account. "Hopefully, you're right. Thank you for your time," she said by way of parting.

Once she and Cody were outside, she glanced in his direction. He hadn't said anything except for goodbye. Curious as to how he felt about what he had just heard, she decided to prod him a little.

"Well, what do you think?" Skylar asked Carrie's twin.

"I think," the deputy began slowly, "that this Brent uses his looks to worm his way into women's confidence, then goes from there."

Cody appeared rather angry to her. She paused next to the Crown Victoria's driver's-side door, studying the deputy's expression.

"There's something more, isn't there?" she guessed.

His expression darkened. "I'm not used to Carrie being so naive," he confessed. "She was always a great deal more savvy about things than this picture her friend painted."

"Maybe your sister was just lonely," Skylar suggested. "Loneliness makes people do things they normally wouldn't have ever dreamed of doing."

"If she was lonely, she could have called me," Cody complained.

She knew that it was Cody's sense of helplessness talking. Skylar unlocked her vehicle. "Sometimes a big brother—or twin brother—just isn't enough," she pointed out.

She could see how the interview with Carrie's friend had really disturbed him. She only knew one way around that for now. "Okay, let's get this photograph and the sparse information we did manage to collect over to Valri," she encouraged. "Maybe she can come up with something more concrete for us to work with. Fingers crossed," she added, holding both of her hands up in the air and crossing her fingers.

He looked at her hands. "You're not planning on driving that way, are you?" Cody asked.

Amusement curved her lips as she asked the deputy, "Where's your spirit of adventure?"

"I left it back in Kiowa," he told Skylar.

She looked at him and saw the distress in the deputy's eyes.

No, he hadn't, she couldn't help thinking. The only way Cody Cassidy was going to be able to deal with this situation was if, somehow, they were able to find the person who'd cost his sister her life.

"I'll help you find it," she promised. She was referring to his sense of humor, which had eluded him.

Skylar drove to the police station. She was figuratively keeping her fingers crossed that Valri wasn't incredibly swamped, that she could find the time to help them locate Masterson—if that was indeed the man's name.

It took Valri Cavanaugh Brody several minutes before she even raised her eyes to see which of the APD detectives had walked in and was standing near her desk, waiting to get her attention.

When she did glance up, she didn't seem surprised to see Skylar and the New Mexican deputy. A soft look rose to her eyes.

"And here I thought that you'd forgotten all about me," Valri marveled.

"Oh, that would never happen, Valri," Skylar told the computer expert in all seriousness.

A weary expression slipped over Valri's face. "That's what I was afraid of," she murmured under her breath. "Talk faster, Skylar. I'm about two days behind in my work and I'm sinking fast."

If that was actually true, Skylar thought, Valri would never bring herself to admit it. She prided herself on staying on top of things, not sinking beneath them.

"I have great faith in you, Valri," Skylar said, "and I need you to locate this man for me." The detective held up her phone, displaying the photograph Carrie's friend had provided for them.

Valri looked at the photo, then raised her eyes toward Skylar and the deputy. "And who is this?"

"Brent Masterson. Could just be an innocent man caught up in something that at the very least is shaping up to be a melodrama," Skylar answered. "Or he could be a murderer."

Valri frowned. "That's pretty widespread." Her glance swept over Skylar. "Which way are you leaning?"

"I honestly don't know," Skylar admitted. "But I need to."

Valri nodded, then looked at the man standing beside Skylar. "And this is…?"

Cody leaned forward, shaking the hand of the woman that everyone thought of as a computer wizard. "I'm Deputy Cody Cassidy. Carrie Cassidy's brother."

Valri nodded, looking genuinely saddened. "I

am very sorry for your loss, Deputy." Those words always sounded so hollow to her, even though she sincerely meant them. Her thoughts turned so something far more useful. "You wouldn't have a copy of this man's fingerprints, would you?"

Cody shook his head. "No, just his name, which may or may not be his real identity," he told her quite honestly.

"Give it to me," Valri prompted. "I'll see what I can come up with."

He wasn't holding out much hope, but he was aware that miracles had been performed with much less to go on, and at this point, Cody felt that he was way overdue for a miracle. If nothing else, he owed it to his sister.

"Any shred of information or evidence will be greatly appreciated," he told her.

Valri inclined her head. "Duly noted," she acknowledged.

At her urging, they left the department's tech wizard to her work and walked out of the computer lab.

"All right, now what?" Cody asked as he made his way over to the elevator with Skylar.

"Now we go get something to eat—" she stared at him "—and don't give me that garbage about you not being hungry. Unless you're a robot, you're hungry," she told Cody sharply. "And after I'm satisfied that I got you to eat some decent food, I need to stop at the hospital. I want to get an update on Rio's wife."

The latter struck him as being rather odd. "Couldn't that be done with a phone call?" Cody asked.

"It could," she agreed, then told him, "But that's not how I do things."

Cody turned the information over in his head. "So I take it that you're a believer in 'trust no one'?"

"No," she said, denying his flippant assumption. "I'm a believer in seeing things with my own eyes. I don't want to bombard Rio with a bunch of questions at a time like this. I am, however, a firm believer in that old saying 'trust but verify.'"

He thought about that for a second, then said, "Fair enough."

Since he wasn't giving her a hard time about it, she felt she needed to sweeten the pot just a little. "I'll drop you off before I swing by the hospital," Skylar promised.

"No need. I can come with you," he told her. "After all, you spent all this time accompanying me while I tried to locate the answers I needed, the least I can do is return the favor. As a matter of fact—" he thought the situation over "—we can go to the hospital before you take me back to my car."

"You skipped a step," Skylar told him.

Getting into the vehicle, he looked at her, puzzled. "Excuse me?"

"You jumped right over the part where you're going to be getting dinner," she pointed out.

"No, I didn't," he contradicted. "I'm not hungry."

"We've already gone around that part. It didn't hold any water the first time and it's not holding any now," Skylar told him. "As a matter of fact, you can pick whatever restaurant—or fast-food place—you want to go to, but you *are* going to go to one," she informed him firmly.

"You know, you really should have some kids so you have someone to order around. Little people who are bound to obey you—until they get older—like five," Cody commented.

"Okay, I'll keep that in mind," she replied. "But for now, you still have to have some sort of dinner."

"You're not going to stop until I do, are you?" he asked her.

She smiled at him in obvious satisfaction. "Now you're getting it," she told him. "Just pick a place."

He sighed. "You can pick the place."

Skylar shook her head as they exited the parking lot. "That's not the point. You have to choose."

"Fine," he snapped. "I'll pick."

The man sounded far from happy. Even so, she flashed a grin at him. "Atta boy. I knew you would come around."

He decided that it was safer not to make a comment on that.

Chapter 11

Ultimately, Skylar brought Cody to her favorite restaurant, Mangia! Very simply translated, the single word meant "eat." It was a homey-looking little Italian restaurant that boasted more than reasonable prices. The atmosphere was extremely welcoming. And as far as the food went, it was very, very good.

The latter piece of information turned out to be Skylar's way of selling the restaurant to the deputy. He still looked rather reluctant about the whole idea of eating anything at all, but in the end, the deputy from New Mexico finally surrendered and gave in.

The owner, Antonio Gaspare, had a habit of welcoming each and every customer who crossed his threshold. The warmth that was displayed was something not lost on Cody.

Standing behind another pair of customers, Cody looked at the woman who had brought him there and asked, "Is this a slow night?"

Skylar looked at him, wondering if the deputy had suddenly lost his ability to see for some reason. She gestured around the restaurant. "Does it *look* like a slow night?" she asked him in disbelief. A number of customers were lining up behind them.

Cody could easily see that it wasn't. "I suppose not," he told her. "But then why is the owner—"

"Mr. Gaspare," she prompted. The man's name was written beneath the restaurant's name.

"Why is Mr. Gaspare going out of his way greeting everyone like this?" He would have assumed that the man would have been better off being at the reservation desk.

Skylar smiled fondly, looking at the owner. "I guess he's just a very friendly man. And he learned a long time ago that if he treated everyone like family, they'll come back—as long as the food is good and the prices are reasonable," she added, knowing that was always the bottom line.

The next moment, the smiling older man had made his way over to Skylar and her friend. Embracing Skylar, the restaurant owner declared, "Ah, Detective Sky, so nice to see you again. You honor us with your presence," Mr. Gaspare enthused. Stepping back, he enveloped her hand in both of his. And then the restaurant owner turned toward Cody. "And who is this?"

The way he asked, it sounded as if he was genuinely interested in the man who had accompanied the detective into his restaurant.

Skylar happily answered his question. "This is Deputy Cassidy. We're working on a case together," she told the restaurant owner evasively.

Antonio Gaspare nodded as he told the young man with Skylar, "You could not have chosen a better, smarter person to work with." He smiled broadly at the young woman. "Detective Sky is a very hard worker and she is very dedicated. I know this for a fact," he told Cody, winking at him. "Come," he urged the duo, "my best table has just opened up."

"Mr. Gaspare," Skylar said with a laugh. "You and I both know that *all* your tables are your best table," she told the restaurant owner.

Genuinely amused, the older man chuckled. "This is why you are always such a welcome sight here, Detective Sky."

With that, the older man guided them to a newly cleared table conveniently located off to the side of the restaurant, creating a feeling of isolation while still being very accessible.

"How is this?" Mr. Gaspare asked as he gestured at the table.

"It's perfect," she responded, then looked at Cody, waiting for him to express his approval. "How about you?" she queried when he said nothing.

Cody nodded, saying, "It'll do," with little to no enthusiasm.

"Coming from the deputy, that's a very heady compliment, Mr. Gaspare," she told the man she had known for years.

The owner held Skylar's chair out for her, then tucked it in as she sat. Handing them each a menu, he promised to send one of his sons over to take their orders when they had made their choices.

Looking on, Cody marveled, "This really is a family business."

She didn't quite understand. "Why would I make that up?"

He sighed, shaking his head. "I don't know."

The deputy really wasn't talking about family business. At least, not *this* family. Taking a guess as to what was really on his mind, Skylar reached across the table and put her hand on top of Cody's, giving it a light squeeze. When he looked at her, she decided that a little positive reinforcement might be what was needed.

"We *will* find whoever's responsible for what happened to Carrie. All of it," she attested. When she saw him quizzically raise an eyebrow, she filled him in on the information that she had left out. "For both her death and the death of the baby she was carrying." She saw Cody stiffening.

The next moment, Skylar found herself very grateful not to be on the receiving end of the dark look that had just crossed Cody's face.

Time to change the subject while she still could, Skylar thought.

"Now you need to put all that on hold for the time being so that you—so that we—" she amended, "can eat something." She knew what had to be going through the deputy's head and quickly continued before Cody could say anything.

"I have known Mr. Gaspare for most of my life," she told Cody. "I am not about to insult the man and walk away before we order dinner, so look at the menu and pick something. Whatever you pick, I promise will not wind up disappointing you in the slightest."

Cody frowned slightly. For a moment, she thought that the deputy was just going to get up and leave.

But then he actually appeared to check over the menu and make a choice, picking out the item that he was the most familiar with.

"I'm ready," Cody informed her in a crisp voice.

Skylar had thought that she was going to have to do more arm twisting, but happily, that didn't turn out to be necessary.

When the owner's youngest son, Marco, returned, ready to take their orders, Skylar exchanged a few pleasantries with him first. Then, pausing, she looked at Cody. She didn't want to take a chance on him changing his mind.

"Go ahead," she urged the deputy.

He ordered a serving of Veal Parmesan, skipping any side dish. When she raised a quizzical eyebrow, he told her with finality, "You wanted me to order something. This is the 'something.'"

"Fair enough," she said. "Make that two orders of Veal Parmesan," she told Marco, surrendering her menu to him.

Marco took Cody's menu as well. He seemed surprised that she didn't order a side dish, either.

"The mashed potatoes are extra special tonight," Marco told Skylar. "My aunt Rosa stopped in for a few hours and my father talked her into whipping up a giant bunch. Everyone loves Aunt Rosa's mashed potatoes. She swears she adds a 'secret' ingredient," the server confided. "You really don't want to miss out on that."

"Okay, you talked me into it, Marco," she told the owner's son.

For his part, Marco looked toward Cody, paused just for a moment and then nodded his head, accepting the man's order the way it stood.

"Coming right up," he promised, withdrawing from the table.

"You're in for a treat," she told Cody the moment that the server was gone.

"I've already gotten my treat," Cody said. "You backed off."

Her eyes met his. "My pleasure," she told him.

Cody had no idea if she was being genuine or sarcastic, but he suspected that it was probably the latter.

He had to admit that he wasn't exactly long on patience right now. "So, what's on the agenda?" he asked after a couple of minutes.

"We eat, we leave, you get some sleep and we start fresh in the morning. With any luck, we'll get something to go on from Valri. In the meantime," she said as she watched their server return carrying a tray with two plates, "you enjoy the best Veal Parmesan west of New York City—or possibly Rome," she amended.

Distributing the two plates, Marco smiled. "I'll tell my father what you said. He will be pleased."

"Shouldn't you taste it before you say that?" Cody asked as their server retreated.

"I don't have to. I eat here whenever I can, and I have *never* been disappointed," Skylar confided. "But you judge for yourself," she urged the deputy, confident that unless he was being perverse, he would agree with her.

Cody took a bite, then told her, "Not half bad."

She almost laughed out loud, telling him, "You do have a way of understating things. Are your taste buds officially dead, or are you just being stubborn?"

He frowned, then took another bite. "All right," he grudgingly admitted. "You're right. It is good."

Skylar got a kick out of the way he all but had to choke out the words. "Now, don't you feel better?" she asked with a wide, amused grin.

"It's going to take a lot more than just good food to do that."

"Understood," she granted. "But at the same time, it is a small first step."

Less than thirty minutes later, as she watched Cody consume the very last little bit of his dinner, Skylar waited for him to retire his fork before asking, "Would you like to have anything else?"

His eyes met hers, seemingly speaking volumes. "Nothing that can be served on a platter."

If this were another time and possibly another place, Skylar would have said that his response practically sounded like a proposition. In all honesty, she found herself almost wishing that it was.

But under the circumstances, she knew that he didn't mean it that way. Cody might not have even been aware of the way his words had come across. With all her heart, she caught herself wishing she had met him before the light had gone out of his eyes.

She had learned a long time ago that wishing didn't make it so. An entirely different set of circumstances would have had to come into being for that to have happened. Right now, the best she could do was to help Cody find who had done this to his sister—and why.

"All right, then," she told him briskly, "I'll let Marco know that we're finished eating. He'll write up the bill for dinner and then we can be on our way."

"I'll pay for dinner," Cody informed her. It seemed only right, he thought, since he hadn't paid for anything yet and she had.

She appreciate his offer, but right now, the cost of dinner was far down on her list of things to take care of. "We'll talk about it later," she told him, then added for his edification, "I have a running tab here."

"I don't care if the tab you have is flying," Cody

told her. "I intend to pay for my dinner—and yours," he added.

"Thank you. That's very generous of you," Skylar replied.

Her tone of voice gave Cody the distinct impression that she was just humoring him, but he wasn't about to argue with her or carry on any sort of dispute about this matter in public. One way or the other, the Kiowa deputy decided, he was going to make sure that Skylar accepted the money for this.

Shifting in her seat, Skylar raised her hand, catching Marco's attention. The owner's youngest son made his way over to their table within a few moments.

"Anything else I can get you?" he asked as he looked from Skylar to Cody.

"Just the check, thanks," Cody answered the server.

"I'm afraid I can't do that," Marco replied, still smiling.

"Why is that?" Cody asked. Anticipating the answer, he informed the young man in no uncertain terms, "This is *not* going to go on the detective's tab."

"No, sir, it isn't," Marco readily confirmed. "My father expressed a wish to pay for your meals." Before Cody could argue the point, Marco explained, "It's my father's way of saying welcome."

As far as Cody was concerned, that was not acceptable. "I can pay for my meal—and I can pay for hers," he stated flatly.

"No one is arguing that, Deputy. But paying for

people's meals on occasion," Marco continued, still smiling, "gives my father a great deal of pleasure."

Skylar placed her hand on Cody's shoulder to get his attention. "You want my advice?" she asked.

"No," Cody answered decisively.

She pretended the deputy hadn't said anything. Instead, she simply told him, "Don't argue with Mr. Gaspare's son. Just smile and tell him thank you."

Turning toward Marco, she repeated the response. "Tell your dad thank-you. Time permitting," she added, "we'll be back soon." Turning to Cody, she asked, "Ready to go? Or do you want to argue some more?"

Cody's eyes never left her face. "Do I have a choice?"

The smile rose to her eyes as she answered, "You always have a choice."

Cody's eyebrows drew together. They had different views when it came to that. The man he had been before coming out here seemed a million miles away.

But he hadn't lost his manners.

"Tell your father thank-you from me," he said to Marco. "The meal was delicious."

Marco looked very pleased. "Thank you. I will be sure to pass that along to him." The owner's youngest son inclined his head at the deputy and then at Skylar. "Until the next time," he told them.

"Until the next time," Skylar echoed, then looked at Cody. "Shall we?" she asked, nodding toward the door.

Cody made no answer, he just gestured for her to begin walking.

She had almost pushed the door open and walked out when her cell phone began to ring.

She and Cody exchanged looks as she retrieved it from her pocket.

Chapter 12

Skylar glanced down at the caller ID number that popped up on her cell phone screen and then looked at the time.

"What's wrong?" Cody asked. After everything he had been through, he immediately assumed the worst.

"I don't know yet," she answered. "Maybe nothing." Or, at least, she fervently hoped it wasn't anything serious.

From his vantage, Cody had already seen who the caller was.

"Do you usually get calls from the computer lab at this hour?" Cody asked her.

"Sometimes," Skylar answered evasively, then pressed the button on her phone, taking the call. "This is Skylar," she announced.

"Hi. I just wanted you to know that I think we might have a handle on who Carrie Cassidy's significant other was. And," she continued, "it appears that the man has a very interesting sideline."

"Well, give," Skylar urged, becoming animated. "Who is it and what is his sideline?" she asked. She could feel Cody's eyes on her, waiting for an answer.

But Valri wasn't about to tell her just yet. "I'll let you know when I can confirm the information."

"C'mon, how about a hint?" Skylar requested, doing her best to get her cousin to come around. Her curiosity was getting the better of her. She was not ready to give up just yet.

"You know better than that, Skylar," Valri admonished her. "Right now, my husband and child have Missing posters plastered all over town with my picture on them. I've got to go home to show them that I'm still alive."

She had heard that song and dance more than once from many members of her family about their particular situations. She knew for a fact that it was incredibly easy to get caught up in the work and forget about everything else.

Skylar wanted Valri to know that she appreciated all the work that her cousin had already put in on the case.

"I do appreciate the update from you. Now go home, kiss that husband of yours and hug that adorable little baby," she advised. "We'll see you tomorrow morning," Skylar promised just before she terminated the conversation.

"So what did she find?" Cody asked the second that he saw Skylar end the call.

"I really don't know," she admitted.

That made no sense to him. "What? Then what was all that about?" he asked, waving a hand at the cell phone.

"Valri just wanted us to know that she was still investigating the evidence and she felt that she was on the trail of something," Skylar said emphatically.

Cody was still waiting for details. When there weren't any forthcoming, the deputy pressed on. "Well, what is that 'something'?"

"Valri didn't want to say anything until she was absolutely sure of the facts," Skylar told him.

"And when will that be?" Cody asked, irritated at the way this investigation was just creeping along and seemed to be going around in circles.

She couldn't blame him for being frustrated. Cody wanted answers. She knew how that was.

"I promise that you'll know as soon as I do," Skylar told him, then felt compelled to explain. "Valri is extremely cautious and thorough. She doesn't like releasing information until she is very sure about it."

"So this is all on hold?" he asked, frustrated about the lack of progress.

"No, it's not on hold, but sometimes Valri has to take a step back in order to recharge and approach the situation with fresh eyes. Just so you know—" she continued "—this is not the first time that she has done this kind of thing."

"And she didn't give you any sort of a clue as to

who she suspects and the kinds of things that she believes this person has been up to?" Cody challenged impatiently.

Was this so-called lab wizard attempting to create some sort of a melodrama for reasons he couldn't begin to fathom?

Seeing his growing agitation, Skylar did her best to calm the deputy, using an incredibly soothing, easygoing voice. "She felt she was getting close and, when she is sure of the truth of her information, Valri will let us know."

Eager to get at the heart of the matter, he asked, "Could I talk to her? I can get that information for her." In his mind, Cody was already interrogating whomever the lab tech suspected. "I just need a name."

He didn't see the problem with that, did he? She supposed that, in this case, it was a matter of not being able to see the forest for the trees.

"That is exactly why she's not about to give you a name. Valri is afraid that you're desperate to bring this person, who might or might not have killed your sister, down any way that you can." Skylar told him what she was certain that he already knew. "We have to go about building this case slowly and carefully so that when we do bring charges against the person Valri suspects, those charges are going to stick.

"For now," she advised, "I'll take you to get your car and then you're going to get some actual rest. You need to be clearheaded, Cody. I promise," Skylar went on, finally walking up to her Crown Victoria, "that Valri is very good at what she does. If anyone can deliver and do what amounts to the impossible, Valri can."

She hit Unlock on the vehicle's key fob and all four of the locks popped up, standing at attention like tiny trained soldiers.

Skylar got in on the driver's side and, starting up her vehicle, pulled out of the restaurant's parking lot as soon as the deputy settled in the passenger seat. Once she was on the road, she glanced in Cody's direction and asked, "Was I right about the restaurant?"

They had already gone through this, Cody thought. With a shrug, he answered, saying, "You were."

"I am also right about this," she informed him. "We get your car, you go back to your sister's place and catch a few winks. First thing tomorrow morning, we go by the computer lab and find out just how much progress Valri has made with the evidence she's uncovered."

This latest turn in the case—the killer's possible identity—had left Cody feeling really wired.

"I'm not going to be able to get any sleep," he told Skylar, then added for her information, "I can go for a couple of days without any sleep."

"Well, I can't," she freely countered. "And since I'm the lead on this case, I vote we go to bed." He looked at her in surprise and she immediately realized how that had to have sounded to him. "*Separately*," Skylar emphasized.

Cody sighed, resigning himself to the situation. A few hours shouldn't make that much of a difference, the deputy silently argued. Besides, he couldn't just waltz off on his own, no matter how much he might want to. If he did, he had no doubt that he could very well get kicked off the case altogether. Being in on this investigation meant far too much to him to risk that happening.

"Judging by the sound of that sigh, you've decided to agree with me," Skylar guessed, barely suppressing a grin.

"Do I have a choice?" Cody asked, less than pleased about the situation.

She didn't bother to beat around the bush. "Nope."

"Then I agree."

Skylar flashed a smile in his direction. "Glad we're on the same page. And, you never know, sometimes a fresh perspective in the morning puts things in a whole new, different light," she told him.

Skylar dropped Cody off by his car at the police station shortly thereafter.

Glancing up into his rearview mirror, Cody noticed that after he'd gotten into his vehicle and set off, the detective began to follow him. He put up with it for a few minutes, but he pulled over about a block later.

"Why are you following me?" he asked as soon as she came up next to him. "I already told you I'm going to Carrie's place. Don't you trust me?"

"Not really," Skylar told him honestly. "This way, if I follow you, I'm sure you're going where you're supposed to be."

"Are you planning on sitting outside the door all night?" he challenged. This woman was unbelievable, he thought.

"No," she answered. "Because if I can't trust you to stay put once you've gone inside, then there's no real point in our working together, is there?"

Cody frowned. In an odd way, he had to agree with her. "So you're putting me on my honor, is that it?"

Skylar nodded. "That is exactly it," she replied.

His eyes narrowed just a little bit. "Did anyone ever tell you that you're one really annoying woman?" he asked.

"Actually, yes," she replied. "My brothers have. A lot more than you." She gestured toward the road. "So, ready to get back to driving to the apartment?"

Cody mumbled something in response, but she felt that it might be better not to ask him to repeat what he had just said.

True to her word, Skylar did follow him back to his late sister's development, then watched as he parked his vehicle and went inside Carrie's apartment.

Rather than drive away, Skylar waited for a few more minutes, then decided to finally leave.

She sincerely hoped that Cody was a man of his word, but she wasn't about to become his babysitter. That definitely wasn't a way to build a working relationship, even a temporary one, she told herself.

Tired, she drove home a few minutes later instead

of going to the hospital the way she had initially planned. But once she walked inside the house, she called to check in with Rio about his wife's condition.

The phone rang four times and, from experience, she knew it was about to go to voice mail when she heard Rio's phone being answered.

Even his hello sounded a great deal more upbeat than the last time she had spoken with him.

"Hi, it's Sky. I'm calling you, Rio, to find out how everything's going. How's Marsha doing?"

Her partner sounded really happy to hear from her. "She's groggy, but she's conscious and she's doing better by the hour. Her surgeon is really happy with the result from the surgery."

She could hear the smile in Rio's voice and was greatly relieved. "So, are you home?" she asked.

"Not yet. Doctor said I could spend one more night here. It makes Marsha feel better," he explained.

In his place, she would have done the same thing, she thought. "Marsha's lucky to have you," she said. "Well, give me a call if you need anything."

"Thanks, Sky. Oh, by the way..." Caught up in his own drama, he had almost forgotten. "How's the search for the deputy's sister's killer going?"

"Valri thinks she might have found the identity of Carrie's boyfriend—and possibly the father of her baby. We need to find his DNA so we can see if we can make a match."

Taking off like that made him feel that he had

dropped the ball. "I'm sorry to have left you in a lurch," Rio apologized.

"Don't mention it. You've got enough on your mind right now," she told her partner. "Give Marsha my best."

"I will, Sky," he told her warmly.

"Uh-huh. Just don't get so caught up in taking care of Marsha that you forget to eat, Rio," she told him.

"You know, you really do need some kids to hover over," he told her.

"There's no shortage on that front," she told him. "I have a whole bunch of nieces and nephews to choose from. Don't forget to give me a call if you need something," she reminded him, then terminated her call.

The thought of having children to take care of lingered on Skylar's mind as she got ready for bed. She had never really actually longed for children, but she had never really discounted the idea, either. For the most part, she liked children and she got along really well with the small people in the family.

However, she wasn't about to run off and have any at this moment. As her mother used to say, *What will be will be.*

Right now—as before—the most important thing on her mind was finding Carrie's killer. She felt that would go a long way to at least partially erase the sadness in Cody's eyes, and that was really important to her. Bringing people like Carrie's killer to justice, to make them pay for their terrible crime, was what she'd been created to do. Anything after that, she thought, came in a distant second.

The following morning, Skylar woke even earlier than she normally did. Getting out of bed, she took a quick shower, leaving it to the cold water to help wake her up and bring her around.

Moving swiftly now, she dressed and, after making and drinking an extra-large mug of coffee, Skylar was behind the wheel of her car.

As she drove to the development where she had left Cody, she mentally crossed her fingers that she would still find his car parked in the space that had been assigned to his sister's apartment.

Because if it wasn't, she didn't have the vaguest idea where to find him. For a moment, she regretted not planting a tracker in his car.

So, when she pulled into the development and caught sight of his car, Skylar breathed a very loud sigh of relief. Cody had kept his word and stayed put, the way she had asked him to.

That was a huge step in the right direction, she thought to herself. Being able to trust him and take him at his word meant more to her than she had believed it would.

Parking in the first space in guest parking that presented itself, Skylar made her way quickly to his door and knocked.

Her knuckles had barely made contact before the door swung open. She found herself looking up at a bleary-eyed deputy whose hair was tousled, looking as if it was going in all different directions at the same time.

"No offense," she told him, "but you look like an unmade bed. Are you all right?" she asked, slightly concerned.

"For a man who got about ninety minutes' worth of sleep—broken up—I'm doing great," he told her, stifling a rather large yawn.

Cody attempted to focus on his wrist to be able to make out his watch. It took a couple of blinks before he was successful. "Is it tomorrow already?"

That was all she needed to hear to make up her mind.

"C'mon, we're going to get you some coffee, and something to eat for both of us," she told him. Skylar left no room for an argument.

He was in no frame of mind to be ordered around, but she did have a valid point.

"Okay."

That was the sum total of his response.

Skylar thought of it as a victory, even though she refrained from saying as much.

Chapter 13

"So, what's the good news, Valri?" Skylar asked the computer wizard as she and Cody walked into the lab.

She placed a large container of coffee on Valri's desk as well as a breakfast croissant, the kind that she knew that her cousin favored.

Valri looked up. The first things that caught her attention were the coffee and the warm croissant.

The computer tech noted with a smile, "I see you've come bearing gifts."

"Just our way of saying thank-you for your efforts trying to find my sister's killer," Cody told the woman.

Valri nodded, her smile broadening. "I see Detective Cavanaugh has introduced you to the time-honored habit of bribery." Momentarily, the computer expert shifted her eyes to Skylar, then she told the deputy, "That didn't take you long."

Valri paused to take a healthy sip from the takeout coffee cup Skylar had brought in, her second one of the morning. "Not bad," she commented, nodding her head at the coffee in her hand.

Unable to contain herself, Skylar finally had to ask, "So, has your hunch paid off yet?" she asked.

Valri looked from one person to the other, not for dramatic purposes, but to prepare them. "Not a hunch, just evidence. From what I've pieced together, your sister and the man she was seeing were very closemouthed about their relationship—but for apparently very different reasons."

Cody looked at the lab tech. "Different reasons?" he questioned. He wasn't sure what she meant, but he gamely went along with it. "What were they?"

Eyeing the deputy, Valri felt her way around her words very carefully. "Apparently, the whole thing about being in a relationship was very new to your sister and she wanted to savor everything within the situation. Her love interest, however, had a far more common reason to keep his relationship with your sister a secret. He was seeing other women. A lot of other women," Valri pronounced.

Skylar saw Cody fist his hands, the only outward sign as to how the information affected him.

"Supposedly, strictly on a friendly basis," Valri continued, "but I have this gut feeling about that."

"And what is it that your gut is telling you?" Cody asked.

"That this guy's 'friendships' went a little deeper than what might have first been observed," Valri told the deputy.

"How deep?" Cody asked in a voice that was far from friendly.

"Not sure yet," Valri answered honestly. "That is one of the things that I need to have to investigated." The computer expert looked at her cousin and Cody. "I figure that's where the two of you can come in—as long as you promise to play by the rules." The latter statement was aimed at Cody.

"What kinds of rules?" Cody asked.

"The kinds of rules that say you can't maim, strangle or kill a person you're in the process of investigating," she said, trying to lighten the situation, but still very serious about the message she was sending to the deputy.

"He'll behave," Skylar promised her cousin. "Right?" she asked, pinning the deputy with a penetrating look.

"Right." There was absolutely no emotion in the single word he had uttered.

To Skylar, that was a dead giveaway. "Cody, I know how you feel—" She got no further.

Cody cut her off. He didn't want to have to listen to empty platitudes that just fell flat, in his opinion.

"You can't possibly know how I feel—" he began but got nowhere.

"I wouldn't take any bets on that," Skylar interrupted. "You don't have an exclusive stranglehold on pain," she informed him sharply. "Now, we're going to conduct a clean, swift investigation and, when we're done with it, the result we come up with will be beyond reproach. Right?" she pressed, her eyes all but filleting him.

Looking far from happy about it, Cody grudgingly admitted, "Right."

Skylar turned back to her cousin. "Thank you for all your help, Valri. By the way, did your little girl know who you were when you showed up last night?" she asked.

A wide smile blossomed on her lips as Valri nodded. "Yes, she did. Seems it wasn't all that late in 'little girl time.' Alex, bless him, was keeping her up for me—not that that was actually a problem. That little girl has her daddy completely wrapped around her little finger," Valri said with a laugh. She promptly took out her cell phone to show off the most recent photograph she had taken of her young daughter.

Skylar looked at the photo more closely. "She just keeps getting prettier and prettier all the time. Theresa is a real little beauty," she told her cousin.

Valri's expression softened as she looked at her daughter's picture again. There was no missing the pride in her voice.

"That she is," the computer expert agreed. "I just wish I could find a way to split myself in half so I could spend time at home and still do my work here." Everyone knew how really important her work was to Valri and how much they all depended on her.

Skylar laughed at her cousin's comment. "If you ever figure out how to do that, promise me that I'll be the first one you tell."

"You've got a deal," Valri answered, adding, "I'll get back to you two the second I get any more information about this guy."

Skylar realized that she had almost walked out of the lab without asking an all-important question. "Well, you could verify the guy's name."

Valri looked surprised and then embarrassed. Apparently talk about her daughter had caused her to slip up. "The guy's name really is Brent Masterson. Word has it that Masterson is currently working as a supplier at the local high schools," she added as an afterthought.

"And what exactly does this Masterson guy supply?" Cody asked. There was no missing the fact that Cody had decided that he didn't care for Masterson.

"Whatever is needed, from what I hear," Valri said. "Currently, he's associated with the local school district. By the way, looking at a clearer picture of the man, he is extremely good-looking. I gather that the guy has half a dozen groupies following him around. Apparently, everyone seems to like him—or is hoping that some of that charm rubs off on them," she said.

"Where can we find him?" Cody asked.

"Well, like I said, he operates out of the school district—but he doesn't stay put for long, so at this point, your guess is as good as mine," Valri said. "He's no longer at the address he listed on his driver's license. The guys moves around, apparently."

Taking in this information, Skylar nodded. "We'll let you know what we find out," she told her cousin.

"Please do," Valri encouraged.

"So, what do you think?" Skylar asked the deputy the moment that they walked out of the computer lab.

Cody sighed in a genuine display of emotions. "I think that I wish my sister wasn't so closemouthed about the guy she was seeing."

"What's your best guess as to why she would do that?" Skylar asked. "Be close-lipped," she explained when she realized that she had left the statement just hanging in the air. "Is it that she thought you wouldn't approve of this Masterson in general, or was she silent for a more specific reason?"

"I really don't know," Cody admitted, even though it cost him to do so. "A couple of months ago, I would have said that Carrie and I could read each other's minds. Now—" He lifted his shoulders in a helpless gesture and then let them drop. "It's almost like I never knew her at all," he said sadly.

"You did," she insisted. "This situation is something that is far more specific," she pointed out. "And by that, I mean that when you're in love, all bets are off."

He looked at her with interest. "You're speaking from experience?" he asked.

Skylar smiled. "I have an extremely large family. I speak from keen observation," she answered.

The elevator came to a stop on her floor. Time to get back to work, she thought.

"Let's see how much information we can gather up about the 'charming' Mr. Masterson," she told him.

But the moment they walked into the squad room, one of the detectives, Mike Martinez, hurried over to her as if he was just about to go looking for her. He nodded a quick greeting at Cody, whom he had met briefly, but his attention was focused on Skylar. "Where have you been?"

"At the computer lab," she answered as she glanced at her watch. "And, anyway, it's early. What's up?"

"The lieutenant is looking for you. They found another body in the lake. No ID on her."

She drew in her breath as she glanced at Cody. "Was she pregnant?" She had no idea what had made her ask that, but her instincts told her that this was just too much of a coincidence for it to stop there.

"Too soon to tell," Martinez told her. "The ME had the body brought in the moment the crime scene investigation unit was finished going over the area." The detective watched as Skylar turned on her heel, ready to go back into the hall so that she could try to get the ME to push up his or her schedule.

"Dr. Richter is on duty today," Martinez told her, specifying the name of the medical examiner who was to perform the autopsy. "You know how thorough *and* how slow he is," the detective reminded her.

"I know. That's why I'm going to the morgue to try to urge the man along."

"Lots of luck," Martinez called after her.

Cody matched his pace to hers. "You think that

whoever threw that girl into the lake is the same person who killed Carrie, don't you?"

"It's a distinct possibility," she answered. "I don't believe in coincidences. And the lieutenant obviously believes it's the same guy, otherwise he wouldn't be looking to hand the case over to me. I'm nothing special," she told him. "There are a lot of other good detectives in this department who could take the case."

"I wouldn't exactly say that you're nothing special," Cody told her, taking her completely by surprise. "Look at how much effort you've put in to working my sister's case already."

As far as she was concerned, that didn't prove anything. "It's my job," she pointed out. "I wouldn't be earning my pay if I didn't give it my best shot."

"Have it your way," he answered, but it was obvious that he wasn't buying her nonchalant brush-off. Despite the hole he felt in his heart, Cody was exceedingly grateful for the effort the detective was putting into this.

She punched the button for the elevator. "I'm beginning to feel I should have my own express elevator, one that goes straight down to the basement and then back up to my floor, so I wouldn't waste any time." Her mouth curved. "That sort of express elevator would shave off at least five minutes when it comes to the round trip," she quipped, then speculated almost wistfully, "Maybe if I'm extra good for Christmas…"

"You could always try running up and down the stairs. That would keep you in shape—" The words were no sooner out of his mouth than he realized his mistake. "Not that you really need to do anything to maintain a better shape. You're great just the way you are."

The deputy seemed to be tripping over his own tongue, Skylar mused. "Is that a compliment, Deputy?"

Cody thought for a second, then answered, "I guess in a way it is."

Her eyes lit up as she looked at him. "Then I guess, in a way, I'm saying thank you," she told Cody.

His eyebrows drew together. "Is that a joke at my expense?" he asked.

In response, Skylar held up her thumb and forefinger scarcely half an inch apart, showing him how small a joke it was on her part.

The elevator came to a stop, its doors lethargically opening. Skylar instantly made a beeline for the morgue. Cody found that he actually had to hustle just to keep up with her.

"I didn't know you could move this fast," he told her, lengthening his stride.

"I can do almost anything if the incentive is right," Skylar answered. She missed the intrigued smile that rose to his lips.

Reaching the morgue, she pushed open the door that led into the area where the autopsies were performed.

"Nobody's allowed in without a specific invitation," Richter growled, barely looking up. But the moment the medical examiner recognized who had walked in, he uttered a deep, heartfelt groan. He still tried to get rid of the invaders. "I'm working here."

"I know." She looked around, trying to guess which drawer Carrie Cassidy was in. The drawers all looked alike. "Do you think you could work a little faster, Doctor?" she requested of Richter. "I need you to perform a preliminary autopsy on the body that was just fished out of the lake this morning."

The medical examiner's scowl merely intensified. "Despite what you might think, Detective Cavanaugh, the world does *not* revolve around you. Each of these bodies gets my full attention when they're on my table. I am not about to be browbeaten to work faster or to work these autopsies out of order. Do I make myself clear?" he asked.

Skylar held on to her temper, even though more than a few choice words rose to her lips. "You've made a lot of things clear, Doctor Richter. Since you seem to be so swamped, I can get you some help."

A short man, Richter drew himself up to his full height, which barely matched hers. "I do not want any help from you, Cavanaugh," he informed her coolly.

She could see Cody growing more and more annoyed. In an effort to keep things low-key, she placed a hand lightly on Cody's chest while addressing Richter.

"It is obvious that you do need someone's help." Her eyes pinned him in place. "I can call in Kristin Alberghetti. She's off today, but she won't mind coming in and picking up the slack."

The medical examiner's face turned a striking shade of red, but he couldn't oppose the suggestion, not since he had already made a point of the fact that he was swamped. "That's your cousin's wife, isn't it?" Richter asked, looking at Skylar.

"Does that matter to you, Doctor?" she asked innocently. "This place is large enough so that you won't wind up getting in each other's way. I just need a couple of questions answered. After that, you take over and conclude the autopsy yourself, if that is what you choose."

Her eyes met the medical examiner's. "Will that be satisfactory to you, Doctor Richter?"

The medical examiner scowled, but taking her family connections into account he was in no position to argue with her.

"All right," he told Skylar. "Call in Doctor Alberghetti."

"Thank you," Skylar responded with a smile that looked extremely genuine to any observer who might be passing by at the moment.

Chapter 14

"There's no such thing as being off duty for a Cavanaugh, is there, Sky?" Kristin asked one of the very first women who had befriended her when the medical examiner had initially attended one of Uncle Andrew's gatherings.

Skylar smiled as she looked at Kristin. "What do you think?" she asked.

"I think that you—and I—are going to be working until the day we both keel over…which, I suppose, is not entirely such a bad way to go," the medical examiner commented. "I had planned on doing that myself, actually."

The detective laughed. "I knew we were of like mind."

"Tell me exactly what you're looking for," Kristin asked the other woman.

Before Skylar could say anything to enlighten the medical examiner, Cody spoke up, answering the woman's question. "What we want to know is if this woman was pregnant when they fished her out at the time of her death, just like Carrie was. And if she was pregnant, would you be able to determine who the father was at this early stage, or is it too soon for you to be able to tell?"

The victim certainly didn't look pregnant, but it was possible because, if this was a first-time pregnancy and this was a very early stage, she could very well not be showing yet.

Admittedly, Cody was going with his gut and playing a hunch.

"Well, if you have a sample of the father's DNA that I can match it against, then sure," Kristin answered. "I can tell."

He had no idea who the father of Carrie's baby was—yet. But there had to be a way around that, Cody reasoned. After all, Carrie's friend Nancy had identified Brent Masterson as the boyfriend. "Could you match a sample of it to the DNA of another fetus?"

Kristin gazed at her cousin-in-law, then back at Cody. It was obvious by her expression that the medical examiner wasn't quite clear what the deputy was driving at. "I'm afraid that I'm going to need more than that, Deputy."

Cody hated going over this, but he knew he had

to, to get justice for Carrie. And right now, that was the most important thing to him.

"My twin sister was pregnant when she was killed," he reminded Kristin. "I don't know the name of the man who got this latest victim pregnant, but there has to be a way to match the DNA from my sister's baby to the one found in this woman—that is, if it turns out that this young woman *was* pregnant when she died."

Kristin turned the words over in her head, then nodded. "What makes you think that this woman was pregnant?" she asked. She hadn't been able to determine that much yet.

Cody shrugged. "Just a gut feeling," he confessed, expecting the doctor to laugh at him.

Instead, Kristin nodded her head. "Oh, the ever-popular Cavanaugh gut feeling," she murmured. "You've been hanging around Skylar too much," she told him. "It's practically a science with these people." Her eyes swept over first Skylar then Cody. "I take it neither one of you has an ID on who this so-called father is? It would make this a lot easier."

"Not yet," Skylar answered. "But we will." There was no doubting the confidence that resounded in the detective's voice.

Kristin nodded, twice as keen on locating the identifying factors now that she was pregnant herself. "In the meantime, I'll see if we can sort through any matches between the dead women's fetal DNA. With any luck, the two DNA samples found with each fetus might point us in some sort of right direction that we can use."

Skylar spared only a quick glance at the body currently on the autopsy table. Anything longer than that and she knew it would definitely affect her. As it was, the sight filled her with a deep wave of sadness. So much potential, all wasted.

"Well, we'll leave you to your work. Give us a call if you find anything or come to some sort of a conclusion, which we can use," Skylar requested.

"Don't I always?" Kristin asked, humor curving the corners of her mouth.

"Yes, you do, Kristin. Yes, you do," Skylar replied with affection. "That's why we requested you."

"'We,'" Kristin repeated. Her eyes smiled as she turned them toward Cody. "Did you request me, Deputy?" she asked, curiosity sparking her interest despite her feeling that she knew the answer to that question.

"Just following her lead," Cody answered, nodding at Skylar.

She was glad he was finally coming around, but her gut feeling told her that their time was limited. They needed to get going. "We have people to talk to and evidence to follow," the detective insisted.

As Cody prepared to leave, he glanced toward the medical examiner. Nodding his head at the woman, he said, "Good luck."

Kristin nodded. "You, too, Deputy," the woman responded as she got back to performing the autopsy.

"What people were you referring to just now?"

Cody asked Skylar the moment they let the door to the morgue close behind them.

"Anyone at the school where your sister worked as a substitute teacher," she reminded Cody. Then she emphasized the fact that Nancy Nelson had mentioned she had seen this alleged boyfriend in Carrie's company before she had left the place. She had gone on to note that he had been exceedingly good-looking.

Cody fought the urge to hurry down the hall. Instead, he held himself in check, Skylar right behind him. "You think this guy she was seeing worked at the school?" he asked, thinking back to what his sister's friend had said.

"I honestly don't know," Skylar admitted. "But we can't totally rule out the possibility." She found herself talking to the back of Cody's head, and lengthened her stride to keep pace. "We have to start somewhere."

"Then let's get started," he told her, still moving fast as he made his way to the elevator.

"Did your sister ever mention any names in passing, anyone she was close to or friendly with?" she asked. They could begin with questioning that person.

He shook his head, pressing for the elevator.

Eternity seemed to pass before it finally arrived. Belatedly remembering his manners, Cody stepped back to allow her to get on first. "Carrie didn't really talk about making any friends at the school. She had mentioned the students she was teaching, how much potential she could see in some of them." He smiled more to himself than at Skylar. She detected a note of wistfulness in his voice. "I felt that Carrie was a born teacher. I never understood why she'd decided to walk away from it to look for another job." He glanced at Skylar, debating if he should say something further. "When I did talk to her, I got the feeling that she was holding something back."

Curiosity immediately crossed her face. "Like what?"

"I don't know. Hence the word *something*," he admitted.

She nodded, making her peace with this non-information Cody had offered. "Okay, back to square one, fingers crossed," she told him as the elevator came to a stop on the first floor. "Let's go."

"To the school where Carrie last substitute taught?" Cody asked.

Skylar nodded and smiled at him. "You're getting good at this."

He ignored the compliment. "So what's the plan?"

"The 'plan' is to talk to every teacher at the school—starting with the ones who have been there the longest—to verify what your sister's friend Nancy told us about Brent Masterson and your sister being together." They made their way out of the precinct and down the stairs into the parking lot. "Any thoughts on that?"

Cody frowned. "Unfortunately, no. Right now, my 'twin' radar is totally failing me."

Skylar sighed as they continued walking toward her vehicle. "That's not the answer I wanted to hear."

He shot her a look, waiting for her to open her Crown Victoria. Tension felt as if it was making its way through his entire body. "Do you have any idea how it feels on this end?"

Skylar unlocked all the doors on her vehicle and slid in behind the steering wheel. She buckled up, looking in his direction. "Frustrating as hell unless I miss my guess."

He laughed under his breath as they set out. There was not even the barest trace of humor in the sound. "Right on the first try," he told her.

Without even being aware of it, he let his guard down. "God, Skylar, I can't stand the idea of never being able to see her again."

Skylar didn't have to ask who he was talking about. She could feel a weight spreading out like icy fingers in her chest as she put herself in his place. It was an extremely heavy weightiness.

It took no imagination whatsoever to know what Cody had to be going through. Her heart ached for him. She knew what she would be experiencing if this had happened to one of her siblings. Skylar was exceptionally relieved that it hadn't, but at the same time, she felt guilty about that sense of relief.

Going with her gut, Skylar pulled her car over to the side of the road. Turning off her engine, she asked, "Would you like a minute?"

"No," he answered in a deadly quiet voice. "What

YOU pick your books – WE pay for everything.

You get up to FOUR New Books and TWO Mystery Gifts...absolutely FREE

Dear Reader,

I am writing to announce the launch of a huge **FREE BOOKS GIVEAWAY**... and to let you know that YOU are entitled to choose up to FOUR fantastic books that WE pay for.

Try **Harlequin® Desire** books featuring the worlds of the American elite with juicy plot twists, delicious sensuality and intriguing scandal.

Try **Harlequin Presents® Larger-Print** books featuring the glamourous lives of royals and billionaires in a world of exotic locations, where passion knows no bounds.

Or TRY BOTH!

In return, we ask just one favor: Would you please participate in our brief Reader Survey? We'd love to hear from you.

This FREE BOOKS GIVEAWAY means that your introductory shipment is completely free, <u>even the shipping</u>! If you decide to continue, you can look forward to curated monthly shipments of brand-new books from your selected series, always at a discount off the cover price! <u>Plus you can cancel any time</u>. Who could pass up a deal like that?

Sincerely

Pam Powers

Pam Powers
For Harlequin Reader Service

Complete the survey below and return it today to receive up to 4 FREE BOOKS and FREE GIFTS guaranteed!

FREE BOOKS GIVEAWAY
Reader Survey

1	2	3
Do you prefer stories with happy endings?	**Do you share your favorite books with friends?**	**Do you often choose to read instead of watching TV?**
◯ YES ◯ NO	◯ YES ◯ NO	◯ YES ◯ NO

YES! Please send me my Free Rewards, consisting of **2 Free Books from each series I select** and **Free Mystery Gifts**. I understand that I am under no obligation to buy anything, no purchase necessary see terms and conditions for details.

❏ **Harlequin Desire®** (225/326 HDL GRQJ)
❏ **Harlequin Presents®** Larger-Print (176/376 HDL GRQJ)
❏ **Try Both** (225/326 & 176/376 HDL GRQU)

FIRST NAME   LAST NAME

ADDRESS

APT.#   CITY

STATE/PROV.   ZIP/POSTAL CODE

EMAIL ❏ Please check this box if you would like to receive newsletters and promotional emails from Harlequin Enterprises ULC and its affiliates. You can unsubscribe anytime.

I would like is to somehow get a lifetime back." He turned to look at Skylar. "Carrie's lifetime."

His dark tone undulated through her. "With all my heart," she told him, using barely above a whisper, "I really wish that I could give you that." She sighed. "But I can't."

"I know," he replied. He hadn't meant to insinuate that she could.

Skylar shifted in her seat, her eyes all but boring into him. "But what I can give you is my solemn promise that I will get this guy who did this to your sister—and to you—no matter how long it takes."

He looked at her then, her words hitting him dead-center. She wasn't just paying lip service, saying the right things. "You mean that, don't you?"

She raised her chin. "I don't lie," she informed him. "Ask anyone in the homicide squad—or my family," she added. "I occasionally bend the truth a little—harmlessly. But I never lie."

Cody had no idea why he found that to be as extremely comforting as he did, but there was no denying the fact that he did. He also caught himself thinking that Carrie would have liked this woman and he really regretted the fact that his sister would never be able to get that opportunity.

Out loud, Cody heard himself telling her, "I'll hold you to that."

His words seemed to suddenly slither up and down her spine, creating an entirely different image than she would have expected being generated by them.

She felt herself beginning to smile. With effort,

she immediately tabled that reaction. Even so, she heard herself telling him, "I'd expect nothing less. Do you want to get back on the road, or do you need a few more minutes to pull yourself together?"

Somehow, although he wasn't entirely sure just how she had done it, she had managed to leech the overwhelming sadness out of his system. At least for now. And, more importantly, long enough for him to be able to tackle finding this worthless scum who had stolen the very breath from his sister.

"Back on the road," Cody told her. There was no room for doubt.

Skylar smiled at the deputy. "Okay, back on the road it is," she told Cody, pulling away from the side of the road.

The woman had a smile that managed to light up a room, Cody realized. He embraced it and took comfort in the effects that smile generated within him.

"You know, I just had a thought." Skylar spoke up as it occurred to her.

"Just one?" he asked, just the tiniest bit of humor reflected in his expression.

"For now," Skylar answered—and then there was humor reflected in her eyes. "There might be more later."

"All right, what's this 'one thought'?" he asked gamely.

"Maybe the assistant principal we questioned the other day about Carrie not seeing anyone was lying."

"Why would she do that?" he asked. Despite the fact that he was in law enforcement—and had had a sister—he would be the first to admit that the female mind was a complete mystery to him.

Skylar shrugged her shoulders. "Lots of reasons, not the least of which might have been fueled by jealousy. You know… 'What does she have that I don't have?' That sort of thing."

His mind immediately went to one place. "Are you saying that you think a jealous woman killed Carrie?"

"That is one possibility," Skylar admitted. But there were others. "Like I said, there could be a lot of reasons that something took place. My mind is open in that respect. But that doesn't make my promise to you any less vital. I intend to solve this, no matter how long it takes."

Those weren't just empty words, Cody thought. Heaven help him, but he believed her.

Chapter 15

They drove to the high school. Ellen Hanks, the assistant principal, looked surprised to see the law enforcement officers walking into the front office again—and she didn't exactly appear all that pleased about it.

"I'm sorry, is there a question that you forgot to ask the last time you were here?" the woman asked.

Cody began to answer the woman's question but Skylar subtly placed a restraining hand on his forearm. She didn't want to get the woman stirred up from the start.

"Last time we were here, we asked to speak to any of Carrie Cassidy's friends," she explained to the assistant principal. "This time, we'd like to speak to all of your teachers, substitute or permanent," Skylar told the woman in as polite a voice as she could manage.

Visible lines popped up on the woman's forehead, forming deep furrows. "I don't see what could have changed, given that the young woman had already left us and, since she is dead, nothing could have changed in that time frame."

Still playing it safe, Skylar felt that Cody's tone could be somewhat off-putting. "It's a known fact that most teachers tend to be more observant than the average person. Maybe one of your teachers saw something they might not have even realized that they observed. You know, an exchange between Miss Cassidy and a male member of the staff, something like that. It didn't even specifically have to be a teacher," Skylar noted. "It could have been a delivery man or a member of the staff, permanent or otherwise." Skylar's voice trailed off as she watched the older woman's countenance. "Sometimes, the slightest thing could lead to a breakthrough."

She could tell by the expression on the woman's face that she wasn't getting through to Mrs. Hanks.

The next words out of the assistant principal's mouth confirmed it as her frown deepened. "This job keeps me far too busy to have any time for idle gossip—"

Skylar could feel Cody growing impatient. She began to talk faster. "I'm sure it does," the detective said quickly. "If we could speak to the staff here, one at a time, in your conference room or your auditorium…" Skylar's voice trailed off as she looked hopefully at the assistant principal.

Mrs. Hanks sighed as her brow creased. "I suppose something can be arranged," she allowed, looking none too happy about her concession.

"We would *really* appreciate it," Skylar told the older woman with just enough conviction to sell her story. Very casually, she laid her badge and detective ID down on the assistant principal's desk.

Ellen Hanks still didn't look as if she was won over, but she seemed resigned to the situation.

"I'll see what I can do," the assistant principal replied.

"We appreciate your understanding, Mrs. Hanks," Skylar replied. "We'll just hang around the school until you can arrange at least a few meetings today."

The assistant principal's face took on an exasperated expression, but it was obvious there was nothing she could do about the situation. The woman gestured toward the seats that were against the wall.

"Why don't you take a seat?" she invited.

"Not exactly the friendliest invitation I ever received," Cody murmured as he followed Skylar to the freshly varnished seats. "But it's better than nothing."

"My sentiment exactly," Skylar agreed, flashing a smile at the deputy.

Cody waited for Skylar to take a seat, then followed suit himself. Seated, he shifted somewhat so that the assistant principal wasn't tempted to read their lips.

Lowering his voice, he asked Skylar, "How do you do it?"

She wasn't sure what the deputy was actually asking her. "How do I do what?" Skylar asked.

"How do you manage to stay so upbeat?" he queried, expanding on his question.

Skylar caught his meaning and smiled. "That's easy enough to answer. The sum total," she told him.

He was furrowing his brow again. Skylar began to feel this was his go-to expression.

For his part, Cody had no idea what her answer even meant. "Come again?"

"The sum total," she repeated. "In this line of work, there are clearly going to be misses. But there are also hits, and I average more of those than I do misses." She could see that he wasn't following her. She tried again. "The hits represent cases I solved and the people I saved and, in the end, that's all that really counts. That's what I shoot for," she explained. "The big total."

Skylar's eyes strayed toward the assistant principal. Mrs. Hanks was making her way over to them. It was obvious by the way the woman conducted herself that she would have been more than happy to send them on their way—but she couldn't.

"Three of the staff can talk to you at the moment," she informed Skylar and Cody.

"What about the others?" Skylar asked.

"They're busy," Mrs. Hanks answered the question coldly.

Skylar played dumb. "Permanently?" the detective challenged.

"No, not permanently," Mrs. Hanks answered, doing her best to mask her irritation. "Just for now."

"But they do know that we want to speak to them, is that correct?" Skylar asked.

"Yes, they know," Mrs. Hanks replied. She glanced at Cody. Unable to contain herself, she asked, "Are you playing the part of the strong, silent type?" There was more than a touch of sarcasm in her voice.

Skylar raised her eyes toward Cody, the look there clearly asking him to hold his peace. She was extremely relieved when he did.

"Trust me, you don't want him voicing his opinion or putting his thoughts into words at the moment," Skylar warned the assistant principal. "You might get more than you bargained for."

Mrs. Hanks began to respond, but there was something about the dark look on the deputy's face that effectively shut her down. The assistant principal backed off for the time being.

Possibly permanently. Her dark brown eyes darted away from the deputy. "Maybe you're right," she conceded.

"Trust me, I am," Skylar assured the assistant principal, doing her best to maintain a friendly expression on her face. "So, where are we going to go to talk to these staff members?" she asked, thinking it safer to assume nothing, not even the positions they maintained.

As a last resort, Mrs. Hanks proposed, "We could do this some other time, you know."

But they'd finally come this far and Skylar refused to budge. "Now would be better."

It wasn't a friendly suggestion, it was an immovable statement.

Mrs. Hanks sighed, resigned. "Now, it is." The woman beckoned to the law enforcement officers. "Follow me."

They did and found themselves in the principal's very small office. The three staff members—teachers, all of them—were already seated inside the room. However, the principal was nowhere to be seen.

Both Cody and Skylar exchanged looks and then eyed the woman who had brought them into the office.

"Where is the principal?" Cody asked.

"Principal Brad Larson is still out sick," Mrs. Hanks answered.

Skylar addressed the woman. "Nothing serious, I hope."

"That makes two of us," Mrs. Hanks murmured. She glanced at her watch. "You have half an hour before they have their next class. I suggest you get to it," she informed the duo as she waved a hand at the teachers.

Mrs. Hanks gave no indication that she planned to step out to give them their privacy.

Cody was about to make that very suggestion

when Skylar spoke up. "We would appreciate some time alone with your staff."

Mrs. Hanks raised her chin. "I intend to stay."

Skylar wasn't having any of it. "Well, unless you're planning on representing these staff members, you can step out," the detective told the assistant principal.

Mrs. Hanks looked far from happy about the suggestion, but she knew she couldn't protest. Looking miffed at being overridden, the woman walked out of the small office.

No one spoke until she was gone. When Skylar glanced in Cody's direction, she noticed that he looked rather impressed as well as almost happy.

Score one for the home team, she thought before she turned to the three teachers. "We assume that you know why you're here," she said, addressing the trio.

Heads bobbed up and down in response.

"This has to do with Carrie Cassidy, doesn't it?" the male member of the group asked. He addressed his question to Cody.

And Cody was the one who answered. "It does. Do any of you know if she was seeing anyone before she left?"

It killed him to be referring to Carrie in such a detached manner, as if he was talking about a victim.

The women both shook their heads, but the male member of the threesome told Cody, "I think she was."

Cody was immediately alert. "Do you know who?"

The teacher shook his head. "Not a clue, but I did see them leaving the school together once." It was obvious he was attempting to pin down a specific occasion. "I think it was just before she resigned from the school."

Skylar couldn't help wondering if one thing had anything to do with the other. Was Carrie worried that she was going to start to show soon, or was she happy about the event?

Skylar pressed her lips together. She needed to get the simpler things resolved before she tackled the larger ones.

"Was the guy you saw with her a teacher or was he just a regular staff member?" she asked.

The man she was questioning, Joe Warner, shook his head. "To be honest, he was kind of far away and I didn't recognize him," the teacher admitted. "The guy *might* have been a substitute but—" Warner raised his shoulders and then let them drop in a clueless shrug.

It was like doing a two-step, Cody thought, frustrated. So near and yet so far.

It went on like that—back and forth—and in the end, no actual headway was made, no real questions were answered. Joe Warner did, however, promise that if he remembered anything at all, he would call the number on the card Skylar had pressed into the man's hand.

"If you want," Mrs. Hanks told the duo, taking pity on them after having come back into the room, "I will address the other staff members today and you can come in early tomorrow morning, before nine, to ask them your questions. Will that be satisfactory to you?"

Her words were addressed to Skylar, but it was Cody who answered her. "That would be very satisfactory to me," Cody affirmed.

For the first time that day, the woman actually smiled. It wasn't a large smile, but it was still a smile.

"We'll be here at seven thirty," Skylar told the woman. "And thank you for all your help. You might very well be helping us to save other young women from experiencing the same dire fate that Carrie did."

Ellen Hanks almost appeared to be preening. "I'll see you tomorrow morning."

"Count on it," Cody promised.

He led the way out of the office and subsequently, out of the school building.

"This sounds promising," Skylar told him as they walked down the stairway. She turned to look at Cody. "How do you feel about it?"

He made his way into the parking lot. Most of the cars were gone now. "Is this a trick question?" he asked. "What do you mean? How do I feel about what just went down?"

Her brow furrowed just a little. He was one suspicious man, she couldn't help thinking. "This wasn't a trick question," she told Cody, enunciating each word. "Do you think we've gotten through to the woman or do you feel that she's trying to lead us around in circles? Because I, for one, think that she's attempting to be straight with us. She might not have any of the answers that we're trying to unearth, but she could very well lead us to the person who does."

Reaching the Crown Victoria, Cody waited for the detective to unlock the vehicle. He heard himself opening up just a little bit. It wasn't his usual custom.

"I really hope that you're right," Cody told her.

"Well, I can't make any guarantees," she admitted, "but I'm crossing everything I can cross in hopes that I *am* right."

He glanced to his left as she started up her vehicle. The smallest of smiles played on his lips. "As long as you're not crossing your eyes as you're pulling out of this parking lot."

"No," she replied, amused. "No eye crossing. I promise."

Exiting the parking lot, she glanced in his direction and suddenly put a question to him. "Are you hungry?"

He actually hadn't thought about eating. Now that he paused to think about it, Cody nodded in response. "I guess I am at that."

"Do you have anything to eat in your—in Carrie's refrigerator?" Skylar asked, correcting herself.

"No. I haven't had any time to go shopping," he admitted. Food was not his first priority, or even close to it.

Nodding, Skylar suddenly turned her vehicle around, practically doing a U-turn. "I have just the place for you to go."

He shot her down before she could get carried away. "I'm not in the mood for restaurant food."

"That's good, because that's not what you'll be getting," Skylar told him, completely losing him in the process.

Chapter 16

Cody looked around at the neighborhood they were driving through. It was entirely residential rather than an upscale district containing shops and restaurants. The deputy kept his silence for a little over five minutes, at which point he decided that he had been patient long enough.

"Exactly where is it that we're going?" Cody asked. As far as he could tell, they were still in Aurora.

She spared him a glance before saying, "We're going to, quite possibly, have the best meal that you've ever had in your life."

He still didn't see anything that even vaguely looked like a restaurant. "I'm not in the mood for riddles, Cavanaugh."

"And I'm not spinning any," she told him in all seriousness. "I just thought you might enjoy a welcome break. But since you seem to be taking a dim view of all this—" her mouth curved in amusement "—I'll tell my uncle not to jump out from behind his stove and yell 'surprise.'"

Cody stared at her, more lost than ever thanks to her glib explanation.

"What the hell are you talking about?" he asked.

Skylar backed up a little, telling him, "You might recall my mentioning that my uncle, the former chief of police, had a gift for cooking."

Cody vaguely recalled hearing words to that effect when he'd first met the detective, but seeing his sister's body in autopsy had wound up blocking out everything else.

The deputy shrugged now. "Maybe," he acknowledged.

Since he didn't stop her, Skylar continued with the story. "When his wife went missing and he wasn't able to find her, Uncle Andrew resigned his position and took an early retirement to raise his five children.

"After his kids went on to join the force themselves, he picked up his hobby again. Uncle Andrew found that he drew great comfort from cooking as he became even better at it than he had initially been. It wasn't long before he began finding a host of different occasions to gather the family together so they could enjoy good food and each other's company." Skylar made a right turn then continued on her way. "From there, it was a very small leap to using any pretext for gathering everyone together."

"That's all very entertaining, but what does any of this have to do with me?" Cody asked.

He still didn't get it, Skylar thought. Her uncle felt very close to law enforcement agents. "You are in law enforcement. You're trying to capture a killer, find your sister's murderer—take your pick." Her smile grew wider as she made another right turn. "Uncle Andrew doesn't need much of an excuse."

Cody put his own conclusion from her words. "I don't need pity," he objected.

"Number one, it's not pity—nor charity, if that's your next comment. And believe me, this will definitely be worth your while. The man knows his way around a great meal."

"If you don't mind, I'll just take a rain check," he told her, thinking that would be the end of it.

But he'd thought wrong.

"No need for a rain check," she cheerfully informed him. Skylar gestured to her right. "We're here."

"Here?" Cody questioned. He looked around both sides of the street.

Skylar had pulled up at the curb right next to a driveway. Gesturing to the two-story house in the background, she stated, "Here."

Swinging her legs out of her vehicle, she began to get out. "C'mon, we don't want to keep Uncle Andrew waiting."

To keep him waiting, she would have had to notify the man that they were coming, Cody thought. "So you called him ahead of time?"

"It wouldn't be polite just to show up," she told the deputy. "Besides, the man has worked—and solved—more cases than we've ever had between us. Who knows, he might have had an experience that can give us insight into your sister's case."

Finished pitching the idea, Skylar looked at him expectantly. "So, how about it? Have I managed to twist your arm?" she asked. Raising her eyes, she saw a shadow approaching through the upper portion of the glass door. "Think fast, because he's heading our way."

Cody was about to say that she was kidding, but then he heard approaching footsteps and knew that she wasn't. Apparently, his time to make good his escape had come and gone.

Cody had no choice but to get out of the Crown Victoria and face the front of the former chief of police's house.

"Smile," Skylar whispered through barely moving lips. "I promise that it'll all be painless," she told him as she got out of the vehicle. "Uncle Andrew!" the woman exclaimed as if the sight of the former chief had come as a complete surprise to her.

Throwing her arms around the man, she hugged him—hard—then began making her introductions. "Uncle Andrew, I'd like to introduce you to Deputy Cody Cassidy. He's from Kiowa, New Mexico."

Andrew extended his hand to Cody, grasping it warmly as he shook it.

"How do you do, Deputy? I've heard a great deal

about you." He smiled as he paused for just a second before adding, "All of it good, I'm happy to say."

Cody was genuinely surprised to find out that the man had heard anything at all about him or why he was here in Aurora. The former chief was undoubtedly just being polite, Cody thought.

Still, the deputy decided to challenge the man's claim. "You couldn't have heard about me, sir."

Cody was about to add that there was actually no reason for the chief *to* have heard about him.

But as Andrew ushered the duo into the house, he told Cody, "I'm the former chief of police, Deputy. I hear everything because everyone keeps me in the loop." His eyes twinkled. "They know if they don't, I won't feed them," he added with a chuckle just before he turned toward Skylar. "Isn't that right, Sky?"

"Absolutely," Skylar agreed. She looked around just as she crossed the threshold into the brightly lit house. "Is Aunt Rose here?"

At that moment, a handsome, vibrant, older woman entered the kitchen from behind the couple. "Of course I'm here, dear. Where else would I be?" she asked.

Coming up behind her husband, Rose slipped her arms around the man and gave him a quick hug, even though she had been in the room with him just a short while ago.

It struck Cody that the two acted more like newlyweds than a couple who had spent more years together than he had lived.

Acknowledging her presence, Cody smiled at the chief's wife. "Hello, Mrs. Cavanaugh, I'm Deputy Cassidy."

The woman nodded. "Yes, I know, dear. Word spreads very quickly around here, faster than you might think," Rose told him. "But my 'source' neglected to tell me how handsome you were, Deputy Cassidy."

"Rose," Andrew said, amused as he called his wife out. "The deputy doesn't know you yet. We don't want him getting the wrong idea about you," he told his wife with a wink. Ever since Rose had managed to turn up and return to him, the woman had embraced life with both arms.

"Sky," the chief continued, "take our guest into the dining area." He gestured toward the area for Cody's benefit. "Make yourself comfortable, Cody— I *can* call you Cody, can't I?" the chief asked.

"You're feeding me, sir. You can call me anything that you want," Cody told the man.

Skylar clearly appeared impressed as she looked at the deputy she had brought to the chief. "I didn't expect that from you."

"And I didn't expect to be invited to the Cavanaugh lair," Cody told her.

"The word *lair* makes me think of people's lives being in danger," Skylar commented on Cody's choice of word. "I'd prefer just calling it the Cavanaugh home," she told him. Skylar saw a strange look cross the deputy's rugged face. "What is it?"

Cody gestured around the wide, open room.

"Where I come from, this wouldn't be referred to as a home."

"What would it be referred to?" Skylar asked.

"It's more along the lines of a small palace," Cody answered simply.

"It's hardly that," Skylar protested. "But we do have a very big family. Over the years, Uncle Andrew has added on several wings to accommodate the various members of the family—not to mention the branch of the family that was discovered, thanks to one of my uncles tracking down the uncle who had been switched at birth. He grew up to have several kids of his own before the mix-up even came to light."

"Don't bore him, Sky," Andrew chided as he came out of the kitchen carrying the brisket he had just finished preparing. Rose followed behind him with the mashed potatoes, gravy and breaded green beans, also all freshly prepared.

Cody shook his head. "She's not boring me, sir," he told Andrew. "To a guy who no longer has any remaining members of his family, this is like being offered a huge serving of dessert."

"You definitely need to come to one of Andrew's impromptu gatherings," Rose told the young deputy. Setting her tray down on the table, she sat directly opposite her husband. "Although I have to warn you, when everyone gets going, you can't even hear yourself think. By the time the evening comes to an end, a little solitude is a very welcome thing," she promised their guest. "Andrew, what do you say?" she asked.

"I'm definitely game," he told his wife. "Spread the word. Is next weekend good for you?" he asked, looking at Skylar.

"That all depends on how far we get with our investigation. Right now, we're at step one," she told her uncle with a sigh.

"Sometimes all it takes is one," the chief said, then amended his statement. "Maybe one and a half."

Beginning to feel more comfortable around this family, Cody laughed softly to himself. "I can see where Skylar gets her optimism from."

Exchanging glances with his niece, Andrew winked. "I get it from her."

"Don't let my husband fool you with his protests," Rose advised Cody. "Andrew here influences everyone. His brothers, his children, and a whole slew of nieces and nephews—far too many to keep track of," the chief's wife told Cody.

"When was your sister found?" Andrew asked.

"According to your medical examiner..." Cody began and then realized that he didn't remember the woman's name. "I'm sorry," he apologized, "I'm not much on names."

He had managed to arouse Andrew's pity. "That's all right, son. There're so many of them, at times I find that I need to keep a crib sheet handy just to keep their names straight."

Rose laughed out loud. "Don't let him fool you, Cody. The man has a mind like a steel trap," Rose told their visitor. "Andrew only pretends not to remember names. He figures that way, whoever he's talking to will not remain as vigilant as he or she might have been at one point." Rose aimed her smile right at Andrew. "Am I right, darling?"

"You are always right, love of my life," he professed innocently.

The conversation over dinner went on like that, continuing a lot longer than Cody had banked on. He also found himself having not just one serving of the brisket, but two.

Stunned, he looked down at his plate. "I had no idea I ate this much," Cody confessed.

"Don't apologize," Andrew told him. "I like seeing a healthy appetite on display. Lets me know I made a meal worth savoring."

"Well, you certainly did that, sir," Cody replied with enthusiasm.

Andrew beamed. "Oh, you are definitely coming to the next family gathering," the chief told Cody. "Now then, tell me about this case you're dealing with," he prompted encouragingly.

Cody sat there quietly for a moment.

Skylar debated leaving the details up to him, then decided to make a judgment call. Her uncle had years of experience under his belt and at this point, they both needed all the help they could get in solving this case. It was the reason she had suggested coming to her uncle's for dinner in the first place. Her intention was to break Cody in slowly when it came to her family.

"Cody came out here because he hadn't heard from his twin sister in two months—with good reason, he discovered," Skylar told the couple at the table.

When Skylar had asked the chief if he'd mind having her and the deputy she was working with drop by, Andrew had placed some calls and had made a point of learning all he could about Cody's back story.

Andrew never liked being caught unprepared.

"Did your sister know anyone in Aurora when she moved out here?" Andrew asked.

"No," Cody answered. "That was the whole point of coming here. Kiowa is a postage-stamp-sized town where everyone knew everyone else. In addition, Carrie was always the one who took care of everyone else. After my mother passed away, Carrie decided it was time that she thought about doing something for herself.

"In order to do that," Cody continued, "she wanted to go somewhere where no one knew who she was. When she read about Aurora in a magazine, she decided that this was the place for her—especially since the weather was so perfect," he added. "We kept in touch, talking every week or so," Cody told the older couple. "In addition, we had that twin-radar thing going." And then his expression grew very serious. "Until we didn't. Whenever I left a message, she didn't call me back. It wasn't like her, and I really couldn't shake the feeling that something was very wrong." He glanced briefly at the chief and his wife. "Sadly," he concluded with a sigh, "I was right."

"Oh, Cody, you have our sincerest condolences," Rose told him.

Cody looked at the chief, then back at the man's wife. "No disrespect, ma'am, but I would rather have your husband's help in finding the person who killed Carrie."

Andrew nodded his head. "You have that, too, son."

Chapter 17

Skylar drove Cody to his sister's apartment.

The trip from her uncle's home to the development where the deputy from New Mexico was temporarily staying was undertaken, for the most part, in silence. She thought it was because Cody was possibly nursing a grudge, or, at the very least, was annoyed at being tricked into attending the small, intimate dinner at her uncle's house.

Consequently, Skylar was in no way prepared to hear the deputy quietly murmur to her, "Thank you."

Blinking, she looked in the deputy's direction, more than a little convinced that she had to be imagining things.

"Did you say something?" she asked, wanting to be certain that she hadn't made a mistake.

Cody took in a breath. She was going to make him stretch this out, he thought. He couldn't really say that he blamed her, given the way he had initially behaved toward her. "I said thank you."

Now he really had her concerned. Skylar watched Cody a little uncertainly. "For what?" Was he thanking her for the meal he had eaten at her uncle's house, or was he thanking her for something else?

She hadn't a clue.

They were almost at the garden apartment complex. Cody knew he had to get this out before he lost his nerve. Apologies weren't customary for him.

"For giving me some hope for the first time since this horrible ordeal all started." He glanced in her direction then went back to staring out the windshield. "I have to admit that, up until now, this all felt rather hopeless to me, like I—we—weren't making any headway in finding out who killed my sister—and why, if there *was* a why."

Well, that made sense, she thought, happy to have been of some help in bringing Cody back among the living.

"Uncle Andrew is going to spread the word, ask around if anyone has heard anything. Aside from being a great cook—or maybe because of it," she amended, "the man has a great many connections in a lot of places. It may take a while, but if we all put our heads together, we *will* find the killer," she told the deputy with certainty, "especially since I have this gut feeling that this man who killed your sister is also involved in other murders.

"Tomorrow," she continued, "we'll go back to the school the way the assistant principal suggested and see if any of the other teachers have anything to add to the information that we've already managed to gather.

"There was your sister and that other victim who was just fished out of the lake," Skylar recalled, going over the information they had managed to pull together. "Killers usually don't change their MOs, so my guess is that both murders were undoubtedly committed by the same person. If we knock on enough doors and ask enough questions, this may all start to come together for us," she told Cody. "At least," the detective emphasized, "we can hope so." Mentally, she crossed her fingers.

Skylar pulled her vehicle closer to the apartment building. She'd intended to keep her motor running, then decided to turn it off just for a moment. She made no effort to get out of the vehicle.

"I'll be by first thing in the morning," she promised Cody, then speculated, "You're probably going to want to use your own car. We can swing by the precinct at that point so you can pick up your vehicle. That way, we can drive to the high school separately." She glanced at the deputy. "You driving yourself over to the school might make you feel better."

Cody had no idea where she was going with this. "Why would my driving my car make me feel better?"

She thought that was obvious. Maybe not. "The

feel of doing something familiar has been known to create a very comforting sensation for a person."

"There is *nothing* comforting about this scenario," Cody informed her.

She supposed that as far as he was concerned, the deputy had a point. Skylar felt rather disappointed that she wasn't able to get through to him.

"Sorry," she apologized. "I was just trying to help."

"I know you were," he told her, feeling somewhat contrite. "I apologize. I have to admit that I haven't been myself since my worst fears came true and Carrie wound up being murdered." Cody blew out a breath. "But I'm working on it. I really am," he said with feeling.

The smile she offered was nothing short of encouraging, as well as blinding.

"I have every faith in you," she told Cody. Her smile widened and spread as she repeated, "*Every* faith."

Skylar had every intention of waiting for Cody to open the door on his side, get out of her vehicle, and then she'd drive away. But she didn't. She didn't have a clue what motivated her to move closer to the deputy, lean in and press her lips against his.

Before she could even begin to dissect her actions, she was already doing it. It was difficult to say which of them was more surprised, Cody or her. All she knew was that the end result felt absolutely exquisite, filling her with a very warm, happy feeling.

When the kiss was finally over, Cody drew back,

staring at Skylar in surprise. And then, clearing his throat, he apologized.

"I'm sorry," he told her. "I didn't mean to take advantage of the moment."

Taken aback, it took her a minute to find her tongue. "You didn't," she finally said, brushing her hand against his cheek and smiling into his eyes. "Why don't we just call it a draw?"

The unexpected smile on his lips went straight to her gut, stealing away her breath. "All right," he agreed. "My sister taught me never to argue with a lady."

Skylar nodded her head. "Your sister was a smart woman," she told him.

Every fiber of her being wanted to kiss him again, but she knew that if she gave in to this overwhelming urge, there was no telling where it might go or, even more importantly, where it would end.

"Well, unless you intend to sack out in my car, I'd suggest you make your way to the apartment. Both of us are going to need to get some sort of rest if we're to make some headway in this case," she told the deputy.

He nodded, finally opening the door on his side. "See you in the morning," he told her. Then, at the very last second, he brushed his lips quickly against hers, before finally slipping out of the Crown Victoria.

He closed the door behind him.

Making his way to the apartment, Cody paused

for the slightest second to look over his shoulder in her direction, then unlocked the garden apartment door and went inside.

He heard Skylar start up her car and pull away. Cody realized he was smiling to himself although, for the life of him, he really couldn't say why.

Skylar could hardly wait for morning to arrive. In the interim, she found herself tossing—turning one way and then another—while sleep continued to elude her. She was convinced that she wasn't going to get any sleep at all and eventually decided to make her peace with it.

Skylar didn't remember falling asleep, but she must have because she suddenly found herself stretching as she opened her eyes. Daylight had begun to creep into her room, blending with and chasing away the shadows.

The first thing she recalled was the sensation that Cody had created within her when he had kissed her last night. She would love to just lay there and savor that feeling, at least for a little while, but there was no time for that. Cody was probably already up, dressed and waiting for her to come by and pick him up.

She definitely didn't want to hear him say something witty about women always being late, especially since she was usually the one who was earlier than anyone else.

Grabbing her clothes, she laid them out on the bed. Showering quickly, Skylar was dressed and ready to go even faster than she usually was. That gave her a little extra time to prepare breakfast for herself and for Cody.

She caught her reflection in the kitchen window and realized she was smiling. Cooking had never held any sort of an attraction for her before, but she thought now that she could easily get used to this if it meant preparing food for Cody.

Get hold of yourself, she warned.

Skylar kept it simple. She made two individual servings of scrambled eggs, toast and bacon. Those she packed separately in plastic containers, then snapped on the lids. She placed the containers into the carryall she had dug up, then made her way to her vehicle.

The whole thing, from start to finish, had taken her less than half an hour.

Skylar drove to the local coffee shop to pick up two steaming takeout cups of coffee, then headed straight for the garden apartment.

Finding a spot to park was a little trickier. It was obvious to her that more people than usual were entertaining overnight guests. Pulling into a spot, she took the carryall and the bag with the coffee with her and made her way to the ground-floor apartment where Cody was staying.

She rang the doorbell. When there was no answer, she rang it a second time. Muttering under her breath, she was about to press it again just as Cody finally opened the door.

His hair appeared to still be wet and he smelled

of some sort of muted bodywash that undulated into her senses.

"You're here," Cody declared with a slight note of surprise.

"Certainly looks that way," Skylar responded, amused as she walked in. Turning to face him, she asked, "Did you have trouble sleeping?"

"How did you—" He wasn't able to complete his question.

"I figured it had to be something like that, otherwise you would have already been dressed and standing outside the door, waiting for me to make an appearance."

He shrugged a shoulder as he took the carryall and bag from her. "Yes," he admitted after a moment. "I had some trouble falling asleep."

"Did you manage to get *any* sleep?" she asked, following Cody into the tiny kitchen. She took out a couple of paper plates, put them on the table, then placed the utensils next to them.

"A little. Enough," he added before she could make a comment about that. He drew in a deep breath as he opened the carryall and took out the plastic containers with the breakfasts she had made. "Smells good," he told her.

"Well, it's not anything like what my uncle is capable of creating," Skylar admitted, "but I promise you won't choke on it."

He laughed to himself. "Good to know," Cody said. "Right now, what I'm really looking forward to is having some coffee."

Skylar gestured toward the containers on the table. "Have at it," she told him, gesturing at both the containers and the takeout coffee cups she had brought. "If it turns out that you don't like what I made, you don't have to feel obligated to eat it. We can stop by a takeout place. I promise that my feelings won't be hurt."

She was surprised that he didn't answer her. Instead, she watched Cody wolf down his portion and wound up smiling. "Either you were *really* hungry, or what I prepared for you wasn't half bad," she said, silently congratulating herself. "You can take your time, by the way. The school doesn't open for another half hour. I just thought that you'd want to be able to eat at a leisurely pace."

"I appreciate that. For some reason, after eating at your uncle's house, instead of getting so full I could barely walk, I just managed to whet my appetite for more food. This was a whole new experience for me," he confided.

"I'm glad I could broaden your horizons," she told him.

Admittedly, part of her had expected to find him less than happy about the questioning they were about to conduct today.

"Are you up for this?" she asked Cody.

"It's something I would have never wanted to face up to," he admitted, thinking that these questions had to do with his sister's murder. "But since I need to, I'm glad that I'll be doing it with you."

She looked at him, mystified by what he had just shared with her.

"Did I miss something here?" she asked. "When we first started out looking into your sister's death and trying to reconstruct what went on, you gave me the impression that you had this huge chip on your shoulder. You actively seemed to resent having me conducting this investigation."

"I did," he admitted. "But I was wrong. You've managed to approach this from a calmer direction. I'm too close to this, and that caused me to lose my perspective. If not for you, I would have."

That couldn't have been easy for him, she thought. But she knew that saying as much would only succeed in embarrassing him. Moreover, it might even cause a schism between them.

"Thank you," she told Cody as she picked up their plates and put them into the trash. She glanced at her watch. It was close to the time that the school opened its doors. "Shall we go?" she asked.

He rose from the table. "Sounds good to me," Cody told her.

"Ready to swing by the police station and pick up your car?" she asked, reminding him that they had agreed to do that first.

"Why don't we just go straight to the school?" he countered. "I don't see any reason for both of us to drive over separately. We can just drive there together. Since our destination is the same, it'll cut down on air pollution," he said with a smile.

Surprised, Skylar nodded. "Let's go," she urged, leading the way to the front door.

"Right behind you," Cody told her, picking up his pace.

Chapter 18

"I have what I believe is some good news for you," Ellen Hanks announced the moment that Cody and Skylar walked into the registrar's office.

Skylar felt her breath catch in her throat, but she told herself not to get too excited. This could all very well just be a red herring.

However, on the other hand, there could very well be something to this.

"We're listening," Skylar responded, waiting to see what the assistant principal had to say.

"Audrey McMillan just returned from taking some personal time," the woman volunteered. "The first thing she asked me when she signed in this morning was if I had heard from your sister. According to Audrey," Ellen continued with what was beginning to sound like a familiar story to Cody, "she had placed a number of calls to Carrie, but your sister never answered any of them." Ellen paused for a moment. The look on her face told them that this had been a very hard morning for her and it was only seven thirty-five. "When I told her that Carrie drowned, she turned very pale and became almost speechless. If anyone knew who your sister was seeing, my guess is that it might actually be Audrey," she told Cody.

Another name, the deputy thought. "And this woman is here now?" he asked, as he looked around the area.

The assistant principal nodded. "I have her waiting for both of you in my office." Ellen gestured for them to follow her.

The moment they walked into the assistant principal's office, the young woman was instantly on her feet. One look at the woman's face, it was clearly evident that she had been crying.

Audrey McMillan brushed the back of her hand against her tearstained face, attempting to dry it.

"You're her brother, aren't you?" Carrie's friend asked. Before he was able to answer her, Audrey told him, "I can see the resemblance. Is she really..." Audrey almost choked on the words. "Really gone?"

It was as if giving voice to the situation made it seem all too real to Audrey. Fresh tears sprang to her eyes.

"I'm afraid she is." Skylar avoided looking at

Cody. "We were hoping you could tell us who she was seeing."

Audrey's eyes dropped and she became slightly evasive. "What makes you think she was seeing someone?"

Skylar could see that Cody was growing extremely irritated. She felt herself becoming increasingly protective of the man. This had to feel like a never-ending nightmare for Cody. She was honest with Carrie's friend—and hoped that Audrey would be honest with her.

"She was pregnant when she drowned," the detective told the teacher.

Audrey suddenly became horror-stricken. Her hands flew up to her mouth to keep the distressed cry from emerging.

It did anyway.

"She didn't tell you?" Cody asked his twin's friend.

Like a robot, Audrey moved her head from side to side in adamant denial. "No—" her voice barely sounded like a whisper "—she didn't. Carrie was very closemouthed that way." Audrey stared incredulously at Cody. "Were they sure that Carrie was pregnant?"

"They were sure," Cody confirmed. "There was an autopsy done," he told the stricken young woman. "Once again, do you have any idea who she might have been seeing?" Cody asked Audrey.

Carrie's friend didn't answer immediately. She stopped to think. "There was only one person she ever mentioned to me," she told Cody. "He's an exceptionally outgoing guy and, just between us, I didn't believe that he was seeing Carrie. At least, not exclusively."

"Would anyone else know if this guy was seeing someone else?" Cody asked. He thought of Nancy Nelson, the teacher who had first told him about Carrie seeing someone. All of this had a very common theme to it. What was Carrie's boyfriend hiding, other than the obvious?

"I was closer to her than anyone," Audrey maintained. "Like I said, Carrie was very tight-lipped when it came to her love life. I certainly didn't know that she was pregnant," the young woman protested. She looked from Cody to the woman with him. "Carrie loved kids. If she was pregnant, I really don't think she would have been able to contain herself. Are you *sure* that she was pregnant?" Audrey asked, still not convinced that was the actual case.

"I'm sure," Cody answered, his tone dark.

Audrey was just beginning to absorb the information, both that Carrie was dead and that she had been pregnant at the time. Her so-called close friend was desperately attempting to make her peace with the information.

"She never told me," Audrey murmured, completely stunned.

"She didn't tell me, either," Cody replied, surprising the woman. "And I used to call her every week or week and a half ever since she moved out here. We shared absolutely everything," he maintained. Then sighed. "Until we didn't."

"I'm sorry for your loss." Belatedly the woman realized that she hadn't extended her condolences to Carrie's twin. She was feeling devastated, but what he had to be enduring had to be a great deal worse.

Cody blew out a breath, doing his best to make peace with the numbness that was traveling inside him. Feeling he needed to say something—*anything*—Cody told her, "Right back at you."

"Do you have a name to give us?" Skylar asked, trying her best to move this along. Maybe Audrey actually did know who this unknown boyfriend was and, for some reason, was trying to shield the person's identity.

"Well, like I said, there was someone she was friendly with, but I didn't think it was anything really serious," Audrey told them. "As a matter of fact, now that I think about it, the guy was kind of a flirt. Good-looking," she quickly emphasized, "but I didn't think there was actually anything really serious going on between them. I think she would have told me if there was. We were friends."

Skylar rolled the words over in her head. "When Carrie didn't let on that there was anything serious going on between them, did you believe that?"

Audrey thought about it and appeared to be on the verge of saying yes, then suddenly denied it. "I really don't know," she admitted. "I'm having a lot of trouble making peace with the fact that Carrie's gone," she confessed.

Clutching her hands together, squeezing and unsqueezing them, she looked from Carrie's brother to the woman who was questioning her. "I thought that Brent was seeing someone else. Like I told you, the man was a flirt," Audrey emphasized.

"Brent?" Cody questioned, repeating the name that Audrey had just used. He wanted to verify that the man was using the same name.

She nodded. "Brent Masterson," Audrey said.

They were finally getting somewhere, Skylar thought, relieved. She could see by Cody's expression that he was feeling the same way.

"Does this Brent Masterson work here at the school?" she asked.

"Not exactly," Audrey told her.

"What do you mean by 'not exactly'?" Cody asked. He felt it was difficult pinning the information down.

"He's a supplier," Audrey told the two people sitting directly opposite her at the table.

"What sort of a 'supplier'?" Cody asked.

"He brings foodstuffs to the school," Audrey told him. And then her voice lowered. "I also heard that sometimes he helps women place their unwanted babies."

Skylar's radar instantly went into high gear. "What did you just say?"

Audrey began at the beginning. "Word has it that Brent would talk women into letting him find a loving home for their children."

"Sounds like the man's a saint," Skylar commented sarcastically.

She looked directly at Audrey. "Tell me, what do

you think of this Brent Masterson?" she asked. Pinning the woman with a piercing look, she added, "Honestly."

Audrey thought her answer over for a moment. "I think he has a silver tongue and I got the impression that a lot of the women he interacted with fell for him."

"Does that include you, as well?" Skylar asked.

The teacher shrugged carelessly. "In the beginning, yes. But he lost interest in me."

That didn't make any sense to Cody. In his opinion, Audrey was an exceedingly attractive young woman. He told her as much in a very matter-of-fact sort of way, then added, "May I ask why?"

She was about to tell the deputy that the answer was too personal. Then, because of her allegiance to Carrie, Audrey changed her mind. "Because I wouldn't sleep with him. He didn't get nasty about it," she told Cody quickly. "There was no name calling or anything like that. He just said that he didn't think we were really all that compatible."

"Would you happen to have his address or his phone number?" Cody asked.

"No, but I'm sure that the principal probably does," Audrey told her friend's brother. "After all, he needs to be able to get in touch with Brent to place his weekly orders."

"When was the last time you saw this Brent?" Skylar asked.

Audrey didn't have to think about her answer. She knew.

"Not for over a week. I was away on leave," Audrey reminded the duo. "And it was just after Carrie made her decision to leave the school."

Skylar exchanged looks with Cody. The timeline that Audrey cited was within the timeframe they were looking at, she thought. "If we need to get in touch with you, do you have a number where *you* can be reached?"

The young woman rattled off a phone number. "If you find out who did this to Carrie, would you let me know?"

"You'll be one of the first to know," Skylar told the young woman.

With that, Cody and she went to talk to the principal.

"I can't believe that that woman could be so naive," Cody said.

"Maybe it's not so much about being naive as it is just not wanting to believe the worst in people," Skylar suggested.

"If you say so. But if you ask me, that teacher, Audrey, was damn lucky to escape with her life intact," Cody said. "I don't think that this Masterson is as blameless as she seems to think he was."

Skylar tended to agree with him.

Brad Larson was at the end of his long, lackluster career. When they walked into his office, they found the principal to be in less than a good mood. Barely glancing at the pair, he waved a disinterested hand at them.

"Unless this is something involving earthshaking importance, I don't have any time to discuss it at the moment," the principal told them. "I've got to locate a food server by tomorrow. The guy who used to make the school's deliveries just up and quit on me and the place he works for doesn't have anyone to cover for him immediately."

"Are you talking about Brent Masterson?" Cody asked.

The principal looked up sharply at the woman and man who had just barged into his office. "You know him?" he asked Cody, about to begin shooting questions at him.

"No, but we're trying to locate him," Skylar told him. When Larson looked at her curiously, she felt that it would save some time if she produced her identification and shield, along with a quick explanation.

Looking over the two identifications, he handed them back. "Why are you looking for him?" the principal asked.

"We thought he might have been the last person to have seen Carrie Cassidy," Skylar explained.

"My sister," Cody put in.

The principal looked up again as if he hadn't really taken close notice of Cody previously.

He did now. "You know, now that you mention it, you do look like her," Larson said.

He had been hearing that all of his life, Cody thought. It struck him with a pang that that would no longer be the case.

"If you talk to your sister, ask her if she would reconsider her decision about leaving the school," the principal told Cody. "She was an extremely good teacher. I hated losing her, especially out of the blue like that."

"I'm afraid talking to her isn't possible," Cody told the principal.

"May I ask why?" He looked from Cody to Skylar.

"I'm afraid Ms. Cassidy drowned." Skylar spoke up, wanting to spare Cody the ordeal of having to go into any details.

The principal looked stunned. After a moment, he found his voice. "I'm very sorry to hear that. Is there anything I can do?"

Skylar immediately spoke up. "You can tell us how much you know about Brent Masterson."

The principal paled as his eyes darted back and forth. "You think that he had something to do with it?"

"We'd like to talk to him in order to rule him out," Skylar said matter-of-factly.

"I don't know how much I can really help," the principal said. "I do know the man was like catnip when it came to the ladies. I can give you his employer's address. I can tell you that Masterson was a really hard worker who had his finger in a lot of pies. But on the other hand, he hadn't been with his company all that long. He hired on about six, seven months ago," Larson recalled.

Turning on his computer, he looked through several listings before he located what he was looking for. Finding it, he printed up the information, then held it out. "Which of you wants this?" he asked.

"We'll share," Skylar informed him before Cody could say anything.

"So he's gone for good?" the principal asked.

"That is what we're trying to find out," Skylar told him.

"Well, if I hear anything on my end," Larson told them, "I'll be sure to let you know. To be honest," he told them, dropping his voice, "there was something about Masterson that just didn't seem to add up."

"What do you mean?" Cody asked.

"He was too friendly too quickly," he told the two people in his office. "You know the type. But then, my wife says I'm just too suspicious."

Skylar glanced in Cody's direction. "Maybe Carrie would have been better off if she had some of that suspicion inside her, too," Skylar said to the woman's brother.

There was no doubt about that. "Maybe," Cody allowed.

Chapter 19

Their next stop was Brent Masterson's former—or present—employer, depending on how Skylar and Cody viewed the situation.

They pulled up in front of a two-story building. The office they were looking for was located on the second floor.

Land of Plenty had been in business for the last eighteen years, delivering food to the local schools, both elementary and secondary.

Cody was the first one to enter the manager's office. The nameplate on the desk proclaimed her to be Alicia Wells. The woman's eyes swept over the duo walking into her office.

"May I help you?" she asked coldly.

"Yes, you may," Cody answered. "I'm Deputy

Cody Cassidy and this is Detective Skylar Cavanaugh of the Aurora Police Department. Could you tell us if Brent Masterson works for your company?" Cody asked.

"'Works for' is a matter of opinion," the woman told the two people facing her desk. Alicia Wells had been the manager of Land of Plenty since its inception. She appeared far from pleased with being faced with these questions. "Why do you ask?"

"Well, we'd like to find out how someone who is employed by your company managed to get involved with helping unmarried young women find homes for their babies, instead having the young women in question talk to their physicians and make their decisions that way," Cody said.

It didn't sound to him as if the two things went hand in hand in any manner.

The manager shook her head. "It was news to us when we first found out about what Brent was doing," the woman admitted. Her voice grew colder. "That isn't what we do here," Alicia Wells insisted. "When I confronted Brent about his 'extracurricular' activity, he said he was just trying to help the young women who came to him. It seems that his name got around for being able to 'help' these troubled young women. But he did promise, once confronted, that it would never happen again."

Mrs. Wells paused, trying to remember details. "That was more than a couple of weeks ago," the woman told them. "We haven't heard from Brent since." She looked from Cody to Skylar. "I'm of the opinion that he quit, but nothing was submitted in writing." Steely brown eyes swept over the deputy and the detective. "Do either one of you have any idea where Brent might have gone?"

"We were going to ask you if you knew," Cody told the woman. This wasn't easy for him to give the manager of the company a reason why he was asking, but he knew he had to explain their presence here. "We think that my sister was last seen in Masterson's company."

The manager looked genuinely distressed by the information. "I'm very sorry to hear that," she told Cody. Her look encompassed both of them. "And you haven't learned anything from the police department?" Mrs. Wells asked.

"We've already told you that we *are* the police," Skylar stressed, informing the woman. Thinking that the woman didn't believe them, Skylar produced her ID and badge and held it up for the manager's benefit. "I'm a detective with the Aurora police department and this is Deputy Cody Cassidy with the sheriff's department from New Mexico."

"When his sister didn't respond to his numerous phone messages, he came out here, looking for her. Aurora was her last known location," Skylar explained.

Having Skylar inform the company's manager why they were here, Cody nodded in the woman's direction. "Your turn."

It was obvious by the expression on her face that

the deputy had lost her. "My turn what?" Mrs. Wells asked.

"From what we can tell, you were Brent Masterson's last known employer," Cody told the woman. "Do you have Masterson's address or his phone number or email address?" Cody asked. In his opinion, it stood to reason that, as his employer, Alicia Wells had to have at least one of those things available to her, if not all of them.

Still seated her desk, Mrs. Wells looked up Brent Masterson's personnel file on her computer, then turned the monitor around so that the two people who were asking her these questions were able to see the answers.

"Yes, I do, but I've never had any occasion to use this information until just this week," she admitted. "When I finally did place the call to him, Brent didn't pick up. He's still not picking up," she confided, none too happy about the admission. "I just tried his number again a few minutes before you walked in." She shook her head. "Still nothing. What I *do* know is that up until this last point, Brent got along with everyone, male *or* female. Especially female," she stressed, pausing as a somewhat wide smile crossed her face.

"What can you tell us about Brent Masterson?" Skylar asked the woman. "Other than the fact that he 'got along with everyone'?" the detective repeated.

Mrs. Wells shrugged, at a loss as to how to answer that question. "That's about it—except that he was a hard worker and never gave me a moment's trouble," she told them.

The woman looked from one law enforcement agent to the other. She appeared to be slightly chagrined as she apologized. "Sorry I can't be of any more help."

Cody looked at the woman, wondering just how sorry Alicia Wells actually was about the matter. She didn't appear all that remorseful, just rather annoyed at the inconvenience. "If Masterson does turn up here, can you give us a call?"

Taking out a piece of paper, the deputy quickly wrote down his cell number as well as Skylar's number below it.

"The top number's mine, the bottom one belongs to Detective Cavanaugh," he explained, nodding at Skylar.

"If Masterson does turn up and I call you, what is it that you intend to do with him?" Mrs. Wells asked.

It might have been his imagination, but the manager sounded rather protective of the man. Cody couldn't help wondering if there was something to that.

He answered the woman as honestly as he could. "I just want to talk to him about my sister, see if he has any information as to what happened to her, who she might have been seeing," Cody said. He wondered if the answer coincided with the one he had gotten from Carrie's friend.

Mrs. Wells raised her head, her tone just the tiniest bit defensive. "She wasn't seeing Brent, if that's what you've heard," the manager said, her eyes meeting the deputy's.

That had come right out of the blue, Skylar thought. "Why would we have heard that?" she asked, the look in her eyes challenging the manager.

"Masterson got around," Mrs. Wells told them. "There was nothing 'exclusive' about him, trust me." She glanced at the phone number the deputy had written down for her. "But I will call you if he turns up on my doorstep, looking to get his job back."

Skylar's antennae immediately went up. "Do you think that he might do that?" she asked.

Alicia Wells laughed softly under her breath, although there wasn't a trace of humor in the sound. "I've learned never to be surprised by anything."

Folding the paper that Cody had handed her, she slipped it into her pocket, once again promising him, "I will call you if he gets in contact with me."

Cody felt drained as well as rather disappointed as they walked out of the building. "Back to square one," he murmured under his breath.

"At least we've confirmed where he was employed," Skylar said.

"The operative word being *was*," Cody pointed out.

"What do you think his placing those unwanted babies is all about?" Skylar asked.

"I'm more curious as to where they came from," Cody told her.

"I think you're a little old to be wondering where babies come from, Cody," Skylar said.

"Want to hear my theory about where those babies came from?"

"Go right ahead, tell me your theory," she encouraged.

"I think this Masterson guy gets women pregnant, then talks them into surrendering the babies, promising to find them all good homes."

Skylar frowned, getting a really bad feeling about this. "Okay, what's in it for him?" she asked.

"Money," he answered simply. "A lot of people are desperate for children. Especially people who might not qualify through the regular channels," he pointed out. "So they resort to less than acceptable channels.

"I have a feeling that this 'irresistible' Brent guy provides his own inventory. He wines and dines these young women, gets them pregnant and then provides them with a solution to their 'problem' that winds up lining his pockets."

It made sense, Skylar thought, but it also made her ill.

"You're making me want to strangle him," Skylar told Cody between clenched teeth.

She noticed that Cody was clenching his hands at his sides.

"Get in line," he told her. He couldn't help thinking about how his poor sister had been used. "If I ever get my hands on this scum..." Cody allowed his voice to trail off.

"You'll blow the case," Skylar told him pointedly, coming to a natural conclusion. "We'll have to proceed slowly with this," she said. "Agreed?"

Cody frowned at what he was proposing. "I had no idea that you were such a killjoy, Cavanaugh," he told Skylar as he got into the Crown Victoria.

Her eyes met his. "You would be surprised how many things you don't know about me."

A slight, ironic smile curved his lips. "Then educate me," Cody told her, placing the invitation before her.

Skylar smiled at him. She was not about to get into that at this point. "All in good time, Cody. All in good time. Right now, we need to gather together all the names of the young women that this supposed Good Samaritan tried to help out."

"Think we can?" Cody asked. "Maybe this so-called Good Samaritan wanted to keep his good deeds a secret in order to protect himself," the deputy suggested.

"This was a school and Masterson got around. People liked to gossip," she reminded Cody. "And women can be jealous creatures if the occasion calls for it."

"Isn't that rather a broad generalization?" he asked.

"I learned a long time ago that the reason generalizations usually ring so true is that they have such an element of truth about them," Skylar told the deputy.

Cody shook his head, genuine sadness in his eyes. "I really wish that Carrie had told me about this slime bucket she had this affair with."

"Maybe she didn't tell you she was involved with this guy was because she knew what your reaction would be when you found out. It doesn't take much stretch of the imagination to know that you would come riding to the rescue, ready to hang this Brent character from the highest tree."

Stopping at a red light, Skylar looked in his direction. "Am I right?"

"Maybe," he conceded evasively.

"Just maybe?" she asked.

"All right, yes," he answered impatiently, surrendering.

"Since we have the possible father's name let's see if we can match his DNA to the fetus Kristin found your sister carrying when she did the autopsy. If we turn out to be right, it'll reinforce our theory," she told Cody.

She placed her hand on Cody's arm and could all but feel the tension radiating there. "I know this part is extremely hard for you to take, but the best thing we can do right now is to avenge Carrie and prove that Masterson got her pregnant in order to sell her baby."

"Then why did he drug her and drown her?" Cody asked.

"You know your sister better than I do. What reason would you come up with?" she asked.

He thought for a moment, and then it came to him. "Because Carrie turned him down when he suggested giving her baby away—especially if the bottom line was watching that baby being sold," Cody told Skylar.

The detective nodded her head as she smiled at Cody. "Give that man a cigar," she declared.

"I'd rather you looked the other way when I find Masterson," Cody told her.

"Sorry, no can do," Skylar told him. "No matter how much I sympathize with you, I want to send Masterson to prison for what he did to your sister, not to mention most likely a number of other young women. The one thing I don't want to do is to have to send *you* to prison," she told Cody. "Now, lock up your temper and help me out here. If you wind up being sent to prison because you avenged her death, Carrie would never forgive either one of us. Understood?"

He sighed. "Understood. But when we finally find this guy, I want five minutes alone with him. Just five minutes," Cody stressed.

Skylar looked at him pointedly. "No," she said firmly. "It doesn't take five minutes to kill a man."

That made him laugh. "Remind me to keep my distance from you," he told her.

"Consider yourself reminded. Losing you would be a great loss to New Mexico and to justice in general," she pointed out. "Understood?"

"Understood," he acknowledged.

"I think we've put in a full day," Skylar told him. "If you're up to it, we can swing by this creep's place to see if we find him in, or at least find something in his place that might implicate him in this 'babies for sale' venture."

"Oh, I'm up to it," he assured her. "Definitely up to it."

"Then let's go," Skylar told him.

Chapter 20

Brent Masterson lived in an apartment complex that surrounded a very fashionable courtyard. Parking close by the actual building, Skylar and Cody got out of the vehicle and looked around the area.

"How does a guy who sells foodstuffs to the local schools in the area afford a place like this?" Skylar asked, shaking her head. "The rent on this place has to amount to one hell of a pretty penny."

"My guess is that he's supplementing his income by placing—or selling—these babies," Cody said.

The words were no sooner out of his mouth than Skylar saw his anger taking hold of Cody again. Attempting to distract him, Skylar nodded toward Masterson's apartment. "Has he answered his phone yet?"

Pressing the phone number on the sheet Masterson's former employer had given them from the man's personnel file, Cody shook his head. "Not yet."

He had already tried to call the phone number twice.

"Then let's go bang on the man's door," Skylar suggested as their next move.

Cody liked the fact that the detective didn't just sit back and wait for things to evolve. "It can't hurt," he agreed.

Approaching Masterson's apartment, they knocked a number of times, but the man didn't answer his door despite how much they knocked.

"I guess we could talk to the landlord and get him to open the door," Cody commented.

"Not without a search warrant," Skylar said. "And to get one of those, we'd need probable cause. Which means bringing the case to a sympathetic judge and getting him or her to rule on it."

"Maybe," Cody said.

He got her attention. Skylar gave him a quizzical look. "What do you mean 'maybe'?" she asked.

"Why don't you see if there's another way into his apartment?" he suggested.

She had already thoroughly examined the door, searching for an opening. "There isn't."

"Humor me," Cody told her as he gestured down the hallway.

He was up to something, Skylar thought. "Just what is it that you have in mind?"

Cody cocked his head as if he were listening to something. "Do you hear that?" he asked her.

She hadn't, but Skylar decided to play along. "Hear what?"

"I can swear I just heard someone calling for help," he told her.

That was the excuse he would use for breaking in, she realized.

"Now that you mention it, I think I *did* hear someone calling for help." Skylar had no sooner admitted that than she found herself watching the New Mexican deputy using his "gifts" to pick the lock on the door.

"Where did you pick up that little habit?" she asked.

Cody looked at her over his shoulder. "You have no idea how many people in Kiowa manage to lock themselves out of their houses and their cars in the course of a year."

Done, he turned the doorknob, pushed it and wound up opening the door.

Observing him as he stepped through the door, Skylar announced, "Brent Masterson, this is the police. We're coming in."

Cautiously making her way in behind Cody, her weapon drawn, Skylar looked around. But to her disappointment, it didn't look like there appeared to be anyone in the apartment.

"Where is this guy?" she asked, voicing her frustration as she scanned the two-bedroom apartment.

"Why don't we go see the landlord?" Cody suggested. "Maybe Masterson gave notice and took off after that second body turned up in the lake."

"You mean when it looked like his perfect gig was unraveling right before his eyes?" she asked.

"Yeah, that," Cody agreed.

"Maybe we can conduct a manhunt for this guy," Skylar suggested. "I can have some of the people on the police force pass around Masterson's photograph as a person of interest, have them try to find out if anyone had seen him. Who knows, we might actually get lucky," she speculated.

Cody appeared to have his doubts about that actually happening. "Aurora isn't exactly a small town."

"True, but the Aurora PD isn't exactly understaffed. If Masterson is anywhere in the city, we'll find him. I can get my relatives to fan out, start knocking on doors and showing that creep's photograph around." Skylar smiled at him, happily informing Cody that, "We are a force to be reckoned with around here."

His eyes met hers. "I'm beginning to see that," Cody agreed.

They went down to the ground floor to talk to the landlord.

James Holder didn't appear overly pleased to have his dinner interrupted. Holder's "What can I do for you?" sounded weary and far from happy.

There was a bulletin board mounted on the wall behind him with all sorts of requests and lists of things from the tenants to address.

Cody took the lead. "Sorry to bother you, Mr. Holder, but we're looking for Brent Masterson."

Holder smirked. "Good luck with that," the landlord told him cryptically.

"I take it from your tone that you don't know where Masterson is," Skylar said as she showed the man her badge and identification.

Holder looked both items over carefully before returning them to Skylar. "Not a clue. Not since his check bounced when he made his last rent payment," he told the duo on his doorstep. Looking from one to the other, Holder asked them, "Did he stiff you, too?"

"I'm afraid the reason we're looking for him is a little more serious than that," Skylar replied. "We're looking for Masterson in connection to a case we're working on," she explained, thinking that might motivate the landlord to answer their questions and help them locate the man. Secretly, she was beginning to suspect that Masterson had more murders attached to him than just two, but she really couldn't tell for sure.

Interest suddenly flared in the landlord's eyes. "Do you mean some woman finally said no to that leering leech?" he asked them.

Skylar glanced at Cody before asking the landlord, "Could you explain that, please?"

"What's to explain?" Holden mocked. "Masterson thought he was God's gift to women and, apparently, most women seemed to think so, too. But I heard one of the tenants recently tell Masterson to get lost. It seems she was really upset that Masterson had backed her up into a corner and was trying to touch her. I turned up just in time to make him leave."

"Do you think we could talk to this woman?" Cody asked.

"You could," the landlord said. "But she took off about a week ago. Can't exactly say that I blame her," the landlord confided.

"You don't, by any chance, have a forwarding address for this woman?" Skylar questioned. She wanted to talk to the woman as much as Cody did.

"None whatsoever," Holder told her. "She paid off her account and took off. Sorry. Now you know the glamour of the rental game."

Skylar's gut feeling suddenly kicked in, front and center. Taking out her cell phone, she quickly went through the photographs until she found one of the second woman discovered floating in the lake.

"This wouldn't be the woman you said took off, would it?" she asked the landlord, holding up her cell phone for his benefit.

Holder squinted slightly at the photograph, then drew the cell phone closer to him for a better look. After a moment, he suddenly cried out, "Yes," surprise all but echoed in his voice. "That's Abigail Juarez." He looked up from the photo, then at the two people standing in his apartment. "She looks kind of pale," he commented, concerned.

"That's because she's kind of dead," Skylar answered.

The man's eyes widened in utter shock. "She's

dead?" he queried as he raised his eyes to look from Skylar to Cody. "What happened to her?"

Looking to spare Cody from having to repeat the story, which was also his sister's story, she simply told the landlord, "She was discovered floating in the lake."

Holden stared at the victim's picture. "That poor kid," he sympathized. "Who was the one who—"

"We're not sure yet," Cody answered, anticipating the landlord's question. "But the ME said she was pregnant at the time of her death. Pregnant, and the medical examiner found fentanyl in her system. It was injected into her arm."

The landlord continued looking at the woman's photograph. "Oh, wow."

"That's the word for it," Skylar agreed. "*Wow. Do you know where we could find her next of kin?*" she asked. To her knowledge, no one had notified the woman's family about what had happened to her.

"She didn't have any, at least not out here. If you find out who did this to her, let me know," Holder requested. "She was a good kid and this shouldn't have happened to her."

It struck Cody that the man sounded really sincere.

"And if this Masterson guy winds up turning up, you call us," Skylar instructed.

"Do you really think he was the one behind this?" the landlord asked, nodding at the cell phone, his meaning clear.

"At this point, nothing is certain. We just have a

lot of puzzle pieces spread out all over the floor," she told him, "and we're trying to put them together to form a visible whole." And then she nodded behind Holder, toward his kitchen. "I hate to tell you this, but your dinner's getting cold."

Holder looked over his shoulder. "I've kind of lost my appetite," he confessed.

They left the landlord with a business card, promising to be in touch if there was anything further to tell the man. Holder said the same to them.

"I had no idea that there were so many dead ends in the world," Cody confessed as they walked back to the Crown Victoria.

She found that she agreed with the deputy, but she took a healthier point of view of the situation. "Eventually, they have to lead somewhere," Skylar insisted as she got into her vehicle and buckled up.

"Why?" Cody challenged as Skylar started up the vehicle.

"Because they just do," she insisted. "This creep is preying on lonely young women, lavishing attention on them and then, when he gets them pregnant, he talks them into giving up their babies—barring that, he steals the babies from them.

"I believe in justice and, somehow, this has to be set right. Otherwise, I've just been spinning my wheels and I'm wasting my time. I refuse to believe that," she told him adamantly.

"Well, I wish I had your faith," Cody said.

She smiled at him, then pressed her thumb against

his shoulder. "There, I'm sharing my faith with you," she told him.

Cody laughed, shaking his head. "You are one very unusual woman, Skylar Cavanaugh. If that's all it took…"

"You just have to believe," she told him, "and it'll all work out in the end. Otherwise, what is it that we're doing here?"

"I'd love to be able to agree with you," he sighed, "but…"

"No one is stopping you," she declared. "C'mon, dinner's on me."

"Are you taking me to your uncle's house?" he guessed.

"No, I think you need some alone time," she told him. "We can grab some takeout and take it over to my place, or to your sister's former apartment. That way, you don't have to talk if you don't want to, but you won't be alone, either."

"What makes you think that I don't want to be alone?" he asked her.

She smiled at him. "That would be because of my 'coply' instincts."

"Your what?" he questioned.

"My 'coply' instincts," she repeated. "All the best cops have them."

"That's a new one on me," Cody told her. "But I do have to admit that you have a way of making me smile."

Her eyes met his as her lips spread in a wide

smile. "Good," she told him. "Now, what are you in the mood for?" she asked him.

You.

The answer just jumped into his head. The next moment, Cody backtracked. "I don't think that's a safe question to answer right now. I'll have whatever you feel like having."

Her eyes met his and then held for a very long moment. In what seemed like an incredibly short amount of time, she felt exceedingly close to him. But she had the feeling that saying so would completely destroy their working relationship.

Deciding to play it safe, Skylar answered, "How does pepperoni pizza sound to you?"

"Filling," he responded.

She nodded. "Filling it is. Next question…" she began.

He wasn't about to get sucked into this or have a long discussion. "Just use your judgment."

"All right, I will. As long as you remember that this was your idea," she told him.

He sighed. "*What* was my idea?"

"Where we're eating," she told him.

"Where are we eating?"

One step forward, two steps back, Skylar thought, resigned. "Your place or mine. Pick one," she reminded him. "The choice is yours. I figured you would welcome having some say-so in the matter."

"All right," he agreed. "Since we're using your car, after we pick up the pizza, drop me off at my sister's place," he told her. "It'll cut down on travel for you."

"Don't worry about me," Skylar said.

"Still, I'd feel better not putting you out," Cody told her.

She supposed that made sense to her. "You got it."

Chapter 21

He had to stop allowing that soft smile of hers to keep getting to him, Cody thought. He could feel it weaving its way into his system.

He blamed it on his being tired as well as overwrought and, yes, even slightly hungry, he admitted.

Cody focused on the warm smell of pizza that seemed to fill every square inch of the inside of the vehicle they were in. It succeeded in further whetting his appetite.

When Skylar pulled her Crown Victoria into the guest parking area in front of his sister's apartment, Cody was the first one out of the vehicle. He took the oversize pizza box out with him. For a moment, Skylar watched the deputy make his way to the ground-floor garden apartment door. Skylar was quick to follow, catching up to Cody just as he unlocked it.

"Maybe we should have gotten two large pizzas," Skylar commented with an amused smile. She nodded at the pizza. "You look as if you could chew right through that box."

Cody glanced in her direction and his eyes lingered on the detective just a few seconds too long. No matter what, it felt as if he couldn't seem to outrun his feelings.

Opening the door, Cody carried in the pizza and placed the closed box in the center of the table.

"I guess I didn't realize just how hungry I was," he told her by way of an excuse. It wasn't quite the truth, but he decided that it would do for now.

"We can always order a second pizza to be delivered if this doesn't succeed in filling your empty stomach," she told him.

Cody laughed dryly. "I'm not a bottomless pit," the deputy told her.

A smile played on her lips as her eyes swept over him. She hadn't been trying to insult him. Quite the contrary.

It was clearly obvious by the expression on her face that Skylar liked what she saw. A lot.

"Not with that trim waistline and those abs of yours," she told him.

His eyes met hers, and once again, lingered appreciatively. "Are you objectifying me, Detective?" Cody asked. For once, there was more than a touch of humor playing on his lips.

"No, not objectifying," Skylar corrected. "I'm just admiring the view," she told him innocently. With that, she opened up the cabinet, then took down two paper plates and proceeded to place them on the table.

For his part, Cody distributed a couple of napkins beside the plates, then raised his eyes to hers. "What would you like to drink? There's one old can of beer in the refrigerator and what looks like a more recent can of soda," he told her. "Both unopened."

Skylar glanced over Cody's shoulder, taking in the near empty shelves inside the refrigerator. "Looks like your sister swore off alcohol and artificial sweetener when she realized that she was pregnant."

Cody couldn't help thinking about the way Carrie looked when her body had been discovered. "That means that she wasn't all that far along before she found out about her condition." He sighed, his frustration surfacing again. "Why didn't she tell me, Skylar?" he asked, turning to look at the detective. "We always talked about everything. *Everything.* I would have never believed that she would keep something like that from me."

Skylar thought she had one explanation for what had happened. "Maybe she kept it from you because your sister was afraid of what you would think of her."

"I wasn't judgmental, if that's what you mean," Cody protested. "Carrie was always the one who toed the line, not me."

"Maybe she was afraid that your opinion of her

would change once you knew about her…shall I say 'transgression'?" Skylar specified.

"It wouldn't have," Cody objected with a deep sigh as he shook his head. "I thought she knew better than that. But I guess she didn't, and now she'll never know."

Skylar stopped eating as she looked at him. "Oh, she'll know," Skylar guaranteed with feeling. "She'll know," she repeated, momentarily glancing upward.

"You believe in that stuff?" Cody sounded more than a little skeptical about faith and what it entailed.

She could tell from the tone of his voice that somewhere along the line, Cody had lost his faith. The man no longer believed, she thought. For all the world, he sounded like someone who had definitely lost his way.

Her heart ached for him.

"With all my heart and soul," she told him, referring to her thought on the matter. "C'mon, Cody. You *have* to believe. If not for yourself," she continued, "do it for Carrie." And then she paused before continuing. "And for you. It would have meant a great deal to her. And, in case you missed this fact, *you* meant a great deal to her."

"How would you even know that?" Cody challenged. "You didn't know my sister."

"No, not personally," Skylar admitted, taking out a slice of pizza and putting it on his plate. She pushed the plate in his direction. "But I have managed to put together the details that you told me about her. And, moreover, I put together certain things I read on her social media page. I couldn't sleep," she explained.

Cody stopped eating and stared at her in stunned surprise. "Carrie had a social media page?"

This was all news to him. He hadn't thought that Carrie was the type to preserve things on her social media page—or even *have* a social media page. It didn't seem like her.

Amused by the stunned look on Cody's face, Skylar's eyes smiled at him. The man could be a complete innocent at times.

"You know, for a really smart guy, you can be such a babe in the woods about some things," she told him.

Cody pushed aside his plate as if he hadn't just been making short work of the slice he had been eating. Like a man on a mission, he rose from the table and immediately hurried off to grab his laptop.

Within seconds, he brought it back to the table. The laptop was over eight years old and took a while to warm up when he turned it on.

When it finally come on, he looked over to Skylar.

He was versed in certain aspects when it came to working the computer, but far from all of them. "What do I—"

Skylar guessed what he was about to ask her. She sincerely doubted that the deputy had ever set up a password for any of the programs on the laptop, which meant that he wasn't able to sign in.

"May I?" she asked, drawing the laptop over so that it could face her.

"Be my guest," Cody told her, gesturing at the laptop.

The moment she got his permission, Skylar began typing. "I'll sign you in," she volunteered just before she glanced in his direction. Belatedly, a thought occurred to her. "I take it that you don't have a social media account?"

Cody frowned as he shook his head. He didn't like being so predictable, but that was really a minor point right now. "I don't have time for that sort of foolishness."

Skylar shrugged. "I'm sure that you have a different way to amuse yourself," the detective suggested, turning slightly so that her eyes could meet his.

Standing behind her, he turned her chair just enough so that their eyes could hold for a moment. "Yeah," he said, answering her question. "I amuse myself by catching the bad guys."

She considered his answer as she nodded her head. "In the sum total of things, I'd say that your way is the better way to go, hands down," she told him as she turned back to the task at hand.

Cody watched her fingers fly over the keyboard. "You have an account," he noted in surprise as she signed in to her social media page.

"Mostly to catch up with old friends. But if this thing disappeared tomorrow—" she nodded at the page she was typing on "—I can't say that I'd miss it."

Finished typing, she pushed his laptop back a little, allowing him a better view of the page she had pulled up and had belonged to his sister.

There wasn't that much on it, but it was enough, she thought. "Carrie was proud of you. Proud of the kind of work you did as a deputy."

He grew quiet for a moment as he not only read what his sister had placed on the page, but eyed the handful of photographs that were on it. "I never knew that this even existed," he confided.

"Well, now you do. And this will stay up forever—unless you take it down," Skylar pointed out.

He grew serious, scanning the pages. "Did she mention that guy, the one who got her pregnant?"

She shook her head. "If he was on here, he found a way to remove his image before you could open the page."

Cody looked through the photographs that remained posted. Some he had never seen before. He realized that this was a way to allow him to keep his twin alive. "I never hung on to photographs," he confessed. "I suppose I just always thought that Carrie would be around forever."

"A lot of us make that mistake," she agreed. "I can print those photographs for you, you know, mount them in an old-fashioned photograph book."

He frowned a little at the suggestion and the image it suggested. "You must think I'm some sort of an old-fashioned throwback," he told her, feeling as if he were completely out of sync with the rest of the world as well as out of step.

Skylar shook her head, dismissing the image he had summoned. "There's nothing wrong with being unique," Skylar told him.

"Yeah, but there's something wrong with being a dinosaur," he corrected.

The hopeless note in his voice hurt Skylar's heart.

Rising, she turned toward him and lightly ran her fingertips along his face, her fingers memorizing his features. "You're not a dinosaur," she insisted with feeling. "You're a really vibrant man with his own unique likes and dislikes."

There was compassion in her eyes.

"I think you're giving me way too much credit," he told Skylar.

"And I don't think you give yourself enough credit. You came all the way out here to find out what happened to your sister and you didn't just go off the deep end. You're making it your mission to bring this guy to justice.

"Now, we haven't managed to track down this scum yet," Skylar continued, "but I guarantee that we will and you bringing attention to what he's been doing is the reason why—as well as the reason why he won't be getting more women pregnant—or stealing and selling their babies," she said vehemently.

He was overwhelmed by the intense feelings that were flowing all through him. Cody laughed softly. "You have a way of saying things…" he told her.

"No," she said matter-of-factly, "I have a way of *seeing* things."

Unable to distance himself from her, Cody framed her face with his hands. Fighting the very strong urge to kiss her.

"I won't argue with you," he told her.

"Good, because by now you have to realize that arguing with me is pretty useless," Skylar responded.

"I've picked up on that," he murmured. There was more than a trace of humor in his voice. And then, as he drew closer to her, Cody lowered his lips to hers.

The intimate contact created all sorts of heat within him. Heat as well as desire. He tugged her closer still—and then, realizing what he was doing and the way he could feel her heart pounding in response, Cody forced himself to pull back.

"I didn't mean to take advantage of you like that," he apologized, searching her face to see how much damage he had done as he began to draw away.

Skylar caught hold of his shirt, holding him in place.

"You didn't," Skylar told him. "Trust me, if you were taking advantage of me, I would be sure to let you know."

Unconvinced—maybe she was just being nice—Cody searched her face. "Are you sure?" he asked uncertainly.

The last thing in the world he wanted was to have her think that he was coming across like Brent Masterson. Cody was still convinced that Masterson had taken advantage of Carrie, and who knew how many other women, in his desire to procreate and then sell those same children to couples desperate for a family. He had managed to satisfy himself, then appeared to ride to the rescue to help distraught, young, pregnant women, and wound up earning money on the side.

"Oh, I am very, very sure," she told him as she threw her arms around his neck.

Finding himself in this vulnerable state with his defenses all but completely evaporated, it was all Cody needed to hear.

When he kissed her again, there were layers of passion surfacing within him, moving in all different directions and weaving through Cody's body.

The more he kissed her, the more he *wanted* to kiss her and the higher the flame burning within him rose.

He knew in his heart where this was going to end, although he told himself that it was going to end differently, told himself that he could control what he was feeling and his reaction to it.

For the first time in far longer than he could remember, he felt something—*really* felt something.

Skylar Cavanaugh made him feel like a flesh-and-blood man rather than someone who was just going through the motions.

This wasn't the time or the place for him to feel this way, Cody told himself, yet there it was, reminding him that he was once capable of caring about a person, like a man cared about a woman, rather than a law enforcement officer who cared about the people whose safety he was entrusted with caring for.

Cody had forgotten what that felt like.

And he had to admit, it felt extremely heartening and invigorating.

Chapter 22

If he continued this way, he wouldn't have the strength or the wherewithal to pull away from Skylar, no matter how good his intentions might be.

"Maybe you should go home," Cody suggested quietly.

Skylar said nothing for a moment, then finally asked Cody, "Do you want me to go?"

He paused for a long minute and then said, "I think you should."

"I didn't ask you if you *thought* I should go," Skylar pointed out, "I asked if you *wanted* me to go."

He had to tell her the truth, even though he knew that it would work against him, and what he felt meant his doing the right thing. "No. Oh God, no," he told her with feeling.

"That's all I wanted to hear," Skylar told him, taking Cody's hand in hers. "Come with me," she urged softly. With that, she began to lead the deputy toward his sister's bedroom.

She could see the doubt and uncertainty rising in the deputy's eyes. The corners of her lips curved slightly. "I promise to be gentle," she whispered.

That was when Cody began to laugh, really laugh.

It was a truly heartwarming sound, but making Cody laugh hadn't been her main intention. "I didn't mean to tickle your funny bone to that degree."

"Oh, Sky," Cody told her, genuinely amused, "you really are something else."

That was practically the nicest thing he had said to her. "Keep talking," she encouraged.

Unable to help himself, Cody began weaving a network of warm, increasingly more passionate kisses along the side of her neck and throat. "I'm not much of a talker," he admitted.

"Then you go right ahead and do whatever you do best," she told the deputy, feeling herself responding and reacting to Cody. "Don't let me stop you."

The feel of his warm breath filtering along the length of her skin created gooseflesh all along her body. It made her desire grow proportionately until she could all but feel her blood heating.

Her breath caught in her throat as she sealed her mouth to his again. A chill went up and down her shoulders and trailed along her spine, causing her yearning for him to steadily increase. Whatever the reason, whatever the cause, Skylar could have sworn she felt electricity shooting off sparks between them.

And then, before she realized what she was doing, she did it.

She was putting her entire heart and soul into kissing Cody.

It was hard to say who was more stunned by the passion that had suddenly materialized, Skylar or Cody.

Or who was more surprised when it happened again.

She hadn't even recovered her breath yet, but there she was, sealing her lips to his a second time, as if to convince herself that the first time had actually happened and that the head-spinning euphoria that took hold of her hadn't been something she had just imagined.

It had to be real, she reasoned, because there it was again, taking her on another erratic-pulse journey, dilating all her blood vessels. It was causing her heart to pound even harder than it had that time she had competed in a 5 K run her first year in college.

Just as she was about to draw back for a second time, she felt Cody's hands on her face, framing it. Holding it as he deepened his kiss and managed to leave his mark indelibly on her soul.

Cody was kissing her as if she was really, really special. And that only made her desperately want to be special—to him.

After a long moment had passed, Cody finally pulled his head back.

Part of him wondered if he had suddenly been catapulted into some sort of an alternate universe. Or maybe he was asleep somewhere and this was all just part of a dream. A very soul-arousing, vivid, wonderful dream.

Struggling to catch his breath, Cody finally gave voice to what he was feeling, "Well, that was certainly a surprise."

"For both of us," Skylar agreed, her voice only a little louder than a whisper.

Taking Cody's hand in hers, she slowly drew him into the bedroom he had pointed out as belonging to his sister.

Once she had crossed the threshold, her legs felt almost shaky beneath her. Lovemaking was nothing new to her, but she honestly had never felt like this before, not even her first time. What was it about this man that spoke to her this way? That made her want him so much?

Yes, he was handsome, there was no arguing with that, but he aroused something within her that went far beyond his good looks.

Get it together, Sky, she silently ordered herself. *If this is meant to be, it will be. If not...well, that was still one hell of a great kiss.*

As if reading her mind, Cody took her back into his arms and started kissing her again, putting his whole heart and soul into that singular, isolated moment.

She felt herself all but melting into his arms, her body pressed against his. She could feel her heart hammering hard beneath her ribs. Sky was surprised that he didn't comment on it, surprised that her heart hadn't just jumped out of her chest.

What was it about this man that spoke to her this way? she silently asked herself again.

"I'm probably going to regret this," Skylar told him in a low, almost melodic voice as she threaded her arms around Cody's neck.

"You don't know that," he told her, closing his arms around her waist and gently drawing her closer to him again.

Yeah, I do.

Skylar thought she had said the words out loud, but maybe she hadn't. Maybe she had just thought them.

But it was too late to find out because his lips were on hers again and there were all sorts of delicious, hot explosions happening inside her at this very moment.

It was too late, much too late, for her to stop herself.

And even if she could, Skylar thought, she wouldn't. Because the truth was, she really didn't want to. At this particular moment, she needed to make love with this man, needed to feel the wild, demanding sensations that she instinctively knew Cody could create within her.

From the moment her lips had touched his, she just *knew* that this was what she had been missing. That somewhere on some lofty plane, it was written that he could satisfy all the needs she was experiencing, all the needs that were throbbing within her.

Her fingers swiftly flew along the front of his shirt, freeing the buttons from their respective holes.

The next moment, she was tugging his sleeves off his muscular arms until he was free and unencumbered by that material.

And as she did that, Cody's fingers drew down the zipper along her back until it reached the end of its journey. Her whole body tingled while the simple shift she had worn today almost sighed as it floated down about her ankles and to the floor.

She stepped from the colorful blue pool her discarded dress formed, abandoning her shoes at the same time. Her breath caught in her throat again as she tugged at the belt at his waist, uncinching it. She felt the hook at her back loosening.

Her bra slipped away from her body just as his trousers did the same from his.

Skylar could feel her skin heating all over again as Cody coaxed her remaining undergarment from her body. Breathing hard, she did the same with his, her fingers gliding possessively along his skin.

And then there were no barriers, no material obstacles left to get in between them.

There was nothing but naked desire to cloak them.

Eager for the final breathtaking fulfillment, Skylar totally expected Cody to take her right then and there. Instead, he took his time, moving slowly.

Making love to her by increments.

Cody pressed a kiss to her shoulders, to her arms,

as well as to the sensitive area of her throat before he systematically moved on to other parts of her body.

Skylar struggled to do the same with him, but it was extremely difficult for her to focus when her head was spinning wildly, like some sort of runaway top.

Heaven help her, but he made her feel utterly beautiful.

And cherished.

And oh so wanted.

She might have been the one to begin this, but he was the one responsible for making the delicious sensation continue.

She tried very hard not to get lost in this burning awareness that was all but completely consuming her, but it was definitely not easy.

Skylar was hanging on to reality just by the ends of her fingertips.

What Cody was creating within her felt almost unreal, like a cherished fantasy that had come to life.

This might not have been her first time.

Or her second.

But it was definitely the very first time she had *ever* felt passion flowing through her to this degree.

And that was what she was going to remember when this all just became a faded piece of yesterday.

She had no idea how many women had been part of Cody's life, if it amounted to an entire squadron or just a few. But whatever the number, she was determined that he would remember being with her like this tonight.

She did things with Cody that she hadn't even contemplated doing until this very moment.

For every caress he bestowed on her, she returned one in kind. For every stroke, every touch, every wild, passionate, soul-melting kiss that he pressed along her eager, pulsating body, she did the same with him, summoning just as much fire.

Or doing her very best to try to summon it.

Lost in each other's arms, they had almost made it to the bed. But some things couldn't be restrained.

They wound up making love the first time on the floor at the foot of the bed.

After covering what felt like every single, pulsing, eager inch of her body with a network of hot, passionate kisses, Cody had drawn his throbbing body along hers.

Watching her intently, he entered her, his hands linking hers just as their bodies formed one joined entity.

As Cody slowly began to move his hips, at first slowly, then with increasingly faster urgency, Skylar felt the explosion within her grow with each deliberate thrust.

And when it came, when that final wondrous climax seized them in its grip, Skylar cried out and wrapped her legs around his torso, holding on for dear life.

Ever so slowly, the incredible feeling receded, leaving her feeling as if she was literally glowing in the aftermath.

But that, too, faded and then reality slowly elbowed its way back in.

Skylar lay there, breathing hard and heavy. And waiting for her pulse to finally begin to level off.

When it did, she expected that now that this exquisite moment was over, Cody was going to say something politely inane, then wait for her to get up, get dressed and leave.

Or maybe he wasn't even going to be polite, just wait for her to leave.

She braced, telling herself that she wouldn't be disappointed, or hurt. After all, she wasn't looking for a commitment, just a momentary diversion, right? If she expected too much, she knew disappointment was only going to be her reward.

Skylar felt Cody stir beside her.

It was starting, she thought. Cody was going to ask her to leave.

To her surprise, he moved over and continued lying next to her on the floor.

He raised himself slightly on his elbow to look at her. "Are you all right?" he asked.

"Yes," she replied cautiously, not knowing what was to come. And then she looked at him. "Why?"

"Well, for a second at the end there, I thought you'd stopped breathing." He wasn't bragging. It was an observation. And then the deputy actually sounded concerned as he asked, "I didn't hurt you, did I?"

This was decidedly a lot more thoughtful than she had thought Cody was going to be.

Swallowing her surprise, she told him, "I'm a great deal heartier than I look."

"Oh, there's no doubt about that," he assured her. "I just wanted to make sure that you were all right."

She realized then that Cody had threaded his arm around her and was now cradling her against him. His heart beat against her chest and she instantly found that incredibly comforting.

"I'm fine," she assured the man who had just managed to totally surprise her.

"Good," he pronounced. Saying that, Cody leaned in closer and pressed a kiss to the top of her head.

He did it as if there was actual affection between them, not just torrid sex that would soon manage to play itself out. Skylar had no idea what to make of that. He was systematically destroying all her preconceived notions about the quiet, morose Deputy Cody Cassidy.

There was a warmth within him that clearly wasn't extinguishing.

This was a whole different person than she had believed him to be.

Chapter 23

When Cody finally rose to his feet, he carried Skylar into the bed, where they proceeded to make love all over again. But this time they did it slowly, deliberately, and with what definitely felt like a great deal of mounting affection, as well as passion.

And when the final moments came and then faded away, they were both in a state of incredible exhaustion.

Cody gathered her in his arms and held her close to him, feeling better and more fulfilled than he had in a very long time.

He honestly didn't remember closing his eyes, and he definitely didn't remember falling asleep. But he must have because the very next thing Cody was aware of was hearing a phone ringing in the distance, intruding into his consciousness.

Opening his eyes, the next morning, he looked around, trying to pin down where the ringing was coming from. When he did, he realized that Skylar had picked up her phone and was sitting up, talking to whoever had called her.

Cody was about to ask Skylar who was on the phone when he heard her asking, "Where?" Responding to the tone of her voice, the deputy instantly became alert.

"I'll find Cody and we'll be there as soon as we can," she told the caller just before she terminated the call.

"Well, you found me," the deputy informed her, spreading his arms out as amusement curved his mouth. "Now, what was that all about?" he asked.

She looked far from happy about what she had to tell him. Putting her cell phone back on the nightstand, she ran her hand through her hair, trying to pat it down into place.

She was stalling, he thought. Why?

The next moment, he knew why.

"They found another body in the lake," Skylar told him. "From all the signs, according to the initial findings by the medical examiner, it looked as if the victim had just recently given birth. She also bore all the marks of having been strangled as well as drowned."

Cody shook his head. "Brutal," he declared with feeling.

"Oh, yes," Skylar agreed. "From all indications, that's what it was."

"Did this involve Masterson?" Cody asked, tossing aside the sheet and blanket that had been covering him.

Skylar had already gotten out of the bed and was gathering up her clothes. "That would be my guess," she told him, "although there's no way to be sure. Yet."

He forced himself to look away even though he still continued picturing her being nude. But keeping that image in his mind wasn't going to help him move this case along, Cody silently insisted. Especially when all he wanted to do was to make love with Skylar again.

It had been several hours since their last time.

"Gut feeling?" he suggested, referring to her comment about Masterson.

Skylar nodded. "Gut feeling."

"Tell me, is that some genetic thing that runs in your family, or is it something that you wound up developing gradually?" Cody asked, curious where this "gut feeling" originated.

Sitting on the edge of the bed, Skylar began to dress. She tried not to notice the way Cody was looking at her, but it was completely impossible not to.

"You're staring," she finally told him.

"I know," Cody admitted. "I have such very few pleasures in life."

Finished dressing, Skylar stood as she stepped

into her shoes. What Cody had just said had made her smile.

"Well, as long as you put it that way…" Skylar watched Cody pull up his jeans and tried her best not to let herself get distracted. Vivid images of their earlier activities were still alive and very fresh in her mind.

Skylar pressed her lips together. "Are you ready?" she asked.

"To see another dead woman?" he stated grimly. "No, not really. But hiding our heads in the sand isn't going to bring her back from the dead—or stop the next woman from becoming another victim."

"My thoughts exactly," Skylar agreed.

Leaving the apartment, she led the way to the Crown Victoria that she had left in guest parking. "I swear," she said, unlocking all four of the sedan's doors, "when we find this guy, it's going to be very hard keeping my hands away from his throat and just ending him."

His expression mirrored her thoughts. "You and me both," he told her. "How does a guy like that get around so much?" he asked. "According to our information, until just recently, Masterson was working."

Skylar had her own theory about that. "There're a lot of lonely women out there, women who feel invisible. Masterson ingratiates himself to them, pays attention to them the way that maybe no one else has. He makes them feel pretty, maybe even desirable and loved, at least for a little while, and they become putty in Masterson's hands.

"When they find themselves pregnant, he tells them about a service he knows of that can place those babies with families that will give them the sort of life that these girls can't begin to give them," she concluded.

"If he offers them that sort of solution," Cody posed, "then why does he kill some of them?"

She was attempting to work that out in her head. "Because at the last minute, maybe they change their minds about giving up their babies. They don't realize that the moment they said yes to giving the baby up, the deal has been struck. In all likelihood, Masterson has already collected the money from whoever he sold the baby to, so he can't let these women back out of the deal. His reputation would be shattered."

Skylar saw the way that Cody clenched his jaw. She knew just how he felt. "As much as I'd like to kill this worthless excuse for a human being, we both know that taking the law into our own hands definitely is not the solution."

"Some of us aren't as convinced about that as others," Cody told her.

She glanced at him as she turned the corner, going toward the lake. "You know you don't mean that."

"Oh, I don't know about that," he said. "If someone had terminated this guy, life would have been a lot better for at least three young women, if not more. This guy is not some Good Samaritan who took a wrong turn, he's doing this for the money, no other reason."

Skylar sighed. "You're right. But that still doesn't

change things. We swore to uphold the law, not take it into our own hands," she reminded him. "No matter how tempted we might be. Otherwise, this would become vigilante justice."

Reaching the lake, she parked her vehicle and got out, making her way toward the section of the lake where apparently the latest body had been found.

Cody reached the area where the crime scene investigators had parked their vehicle. Passing the van, he looked down at the dead woman on the stretcher. In his judgment, she couldn't have been dead for more than six or eight hours.

That had transpired while he and Skylar had been making love, he thought. That hit him hard. Very hard.

He tried not to dwell on it.

Skylar looked down at the dead woman grimly.

"She doesn't even look like she was twenty years old," he noted somberly.

This particular medical examiner, a man named Peter Chambers who had been at this a number of years, pushed to his feet as he turned around. "That's because she's not. This is Karen Wakefield and she isn't going to get to see her nineteenth birthday." Chambers's face turned a dark shade of red. "This guy's a monster who preys on impressionable young women that fancy themselves as being worldly," he told Skylar and the angry-looking deputy at her side.

Chambers, the father of four daughters, looked at the two law enforcement officers before him. "Do the world a favor," he told Skylar. "Get rid of this vermin when you track him down. Do it before I forget all about my Hippocratic oath."

It was Cody who answered him. "Believe me, there's nothing that I'd like more," Cody told the medical examiner with utter sincerity. "But that would wind up raising a whole host of other problems."

Skylar looked at the deputy, a sense of overwhelming relief washing over her. It sounded to her as if Cody was finally coming around about the matter, at least a little.

She turned to another question plaguing her. "What about the baby and how far she was in her pregnancy?" Skylar asked the ME.

"My best guess is that the killer recently cut the baby out of her, possibly in the last few hours. This character has a string of victims and it looks like he knows his time is all but up."

"I certainly hope so," Skylar said with feeling. She noticed that Cody was taking in the surrounding area, specifically paying close attention to the trees surrounding the lake on their side. Something had caught his attention. "What are you thinking?"

Cody slowly looked around. "What kind of reception does this area get?"

"Fairly decent, from what I hear," Chambers answered. "Two of my daughters like to come up here with their friends. I'm told that they record these gatherings of theirs for 'posterity.' I've already told them that they have to stop doing that for the time being. They're not happy about it, but they'll listen," he said. Looking at Cody, the medical examiner asked, "Why would you ask that?"

"Because I'm wondering if we might be able to capture activities on camera," Cody answered the doctor. He looked at Skylar. "What do you think?"

She turned the idea over in her head, surveying the trees. She took them in from a completely different vantage point.

"I don't see why not." Skylar speculated, "We would have to get some battery-powered, motion-sensitive cameras and mount them in several different places, all out of view. But I can't see why that couldn't be done."

Skylar thought of Valri. "I'm sure that my cousin could rig up something for us." As she spoke, her face lit up. It was definitely an idea. "I'll talk to her as soon as we get back and tell her about your idea."

"It's not 'my' idea," Cody pointed out. "I wouldn't have thought of it if the medical examiner hadn't started talking about his daughters."

Cody didn't want to take credit for coming up with any solutions, he just wanted this whole ugly situation to go away as quickly as possible.

"What are you going to do when I go on vacation?" Valri asked as she watched her cousin and Cody walk in. They hadn't even asked a question yet, but she had anticipated that they would.

"Who are you kidding, Valri? You don't go on vacation," Skylar told her. "For all we know, you spend your nights just haunting these halls. At least, there are times when it certainly feels that way."

Valri raised her eyes off her screen. "Okay, what do I need to do to make you go away this time?" the computer tech asked.

Skylar immediately spoke up. "We're going to need your strongest, newest cameras."

Well, that had certainly been unexpected, Valri thought. "I know this is a silly question to ask, but what do you need them for?"

"We want to hang them up inside the ring of trees around the lake. It would be to alert the Homicide Division that another homicide was taking place," Cody told the technician. "At least three bodies have turned up around Lake Aurora in the last couple of days. This guy had upped his game and since it seems to be taking place in the same area, motion-sensitive cameras might wind up catching him in the act," he told her. "My question is, do you have anything that's strong enough and sensitive enough to be able to do this?" Cody asked.

"This way, we can set up the cameras and bring this guy down before he kills someone else," Skylar said, adding her enthusiasm to the idea of catching the guy on video.

Valri smiled. "I just got in some brand-new equipment. I can have a couple of my best techs mount the cameras in the area. With any luck, we'll be able to get this guy before he does any more damage."

"Do you have any way we can monitor the cameras on an ongoing basis?" Cody asked.

Valri looked at the deputy. "I'll pretend you didn't just ask that, Cody."

"Not everyone knows as much about cameras and computers as you do," Skylar pointed out to her cousin. "As a matter of fact, I'm fairly certain that *no one* knows as much about any of this tech stuff as you do."

And then Skylar raised her eyes, directing her gaze toward Cody. "Sorry, I didn't mean to insult you," she apologized.

After the night they had spent together, he was fairly certain that nothing she could say or do would actually wind up insulting him. "You didn't," he told her. Cody shifted his attention to Valri, getting back to the business at hand. "How fast can your people put up those cameras?"

"Fast," Valri answered. "But you don't really expect this maniac to kill again so soon, do you?" she asked.

"We really don't know what to expect," Skylar answered honestly. "We just want to be prepared for any contingencies. That, and to have a monitor that is prepped and ready to pick up any photos in the immediate area. Is that doable?"

"We'll get on this right away," Valri promised, sounding angrier than Skylar could ever remember hearing her. The anger was directed at Masterson. "This maniac deserves to be put down like the mad dog that he is," the tech wizard declared. Taking a breath to calm down, she told the law enforcement officers, "I'll be in touch with you both as soon as everything is ready to go."

"And just when will that be?" Cody asked.

"Pushy, isn't he?" Valri asked her cousin, indicating Cody with her eyes.

Skylar laughed in response. "You have *no* idea," she told Valri, then said, "Be sure to give us a call the minute the equipment is all set up and ready to be used."

With that, she and Cody crossed their fingers and walked out of the computer lab.

Chapter 24

Hoping to follow up on various clues they had managed to come across in an attempt to locate Masterson before he killed again, Skylar and Cody spoke to all the women they could find who had had any dealings with the man who had cost some of the women their babies.

They had been at this for over three weeks now and had made very little headway.

"How can one man be in so many places at once and still remain invisible?" Skylar marveled, disgusted. She felt exhausted and somewhat shell-shocked at the same time as she lay in Cody's arms one night.

Having been placed in the position of either renewing Carrie's lease or moving out, Cody had set out to find another place to stay for the duration until he was able to bring this killer to justice.

It was Skylar who had suggested that Cody remain at her place for the amount of time it would take to locate the killer. Her reasoning was how much longer could it take with so many more detectives on the job now than there had been initially? She had made a whole slew of copies of the photograph that she had managed to lift from the one rather blurry copy that had been cleared up of Masterson.

Consequently, Cody and she had been putting in one fifteen-hour-day after another, all to very little avail. A few times, they had almost managed to catch Masterson, but each and every time, the baby trafficker managed to get away, frustrating all their efforts.

"Obviously, Masterson has been at this for a while now. Probably longer than we initially thought and, rather than be satisfied with all the money he has managed to amass, he's getting greedier."

She ran her fingers slowly along Cody's chest, arousing both of them to a degree, despite the fact that they were both rather tired.

"Masterson—or whatever his real name is— upped the ante, trying to get even more money together before he calls it a day. Not that he ever would," she told Cody. "People like Masterson are insatiably greedy." Resting her head against his chest, she raised it to look at Cody. "But eventually, he *will* make a mistake and this reign of terror of his will finally be over. I just really hope that it will be sooner than later."

Cody's eyes met hers. "And just what will we do until then?" he asked her "innocently."

He was doing it again, she thought. He was looking into her soul with those big green eyes of his and unraveling her. "Oh, I think I might have an idea or three about that," she answered.

"Do I get a vote in this?" Cody asked.

"Be my guest. Vote away," she urged, slipping her arms around his neck as she pressed her lips against his.

Cody could feel his blood heating a little more with each and every kiss.

"That," he told her, doing his best to catch his breath. "I definitely vote for that," Cody said like a man who knew he had lost the confrontation and didn't really care that he had.

"Good call," Skylar agreed, her eyes smiling at him as she curled up even further into his arms.

Skylar wasn't quite sure what woke her up. If it was something in her dream, she had no memory of it when she opened her eyes.

Moreover, when she opened her eyes, she saw that the spot beside her was empty.

Concerned, she got out of bed and threw on her bathrobe. Tying the sash at her waist, Skylar went looking for Cody.

She found him sitting in the kitchen at the table,

nursing a cup of black coffee. It didn't appear to be his first one of the morning.

It was still dark outside, she noted.

Skylar quietly walked into the room rather than call out his name because she didn't want to startle Cody.

"Everything all right?" she asked him quietly.

He turned to look at her. "I couldn't sleep," he told her by way of an explanation.

"So you decided to have some coffee in order to put you to sleep?" Skylar quipped with a soft laugh. "I'm not sure you're exactly clear on the concept of what coffee is supposed to do." Moving toward the coffee maker on the counter, she asked, "Did you leave any for me?"

Cody shook his head. "I didn't mean to wake you, Sky."

"You didn't." She filled a coffee cup with what was left in the pot, then poured in some cream, turning the liquid into a very light shade of chocolate. "My dream did. Although, now that I'm awake, I can't tell you what it was about," she confessed, returning to the table.

"You're lucky. I can tell you what all my dreams were about," he told her soberly.

She didn't have to guess. Of late, whenever he was having a bad dream, she was aware of it. She could hear him moaning in his sleep. She never bothered waking him, she just went on holding him until the moaning ceased.

Right now, she covered his hand with her own.

"We'll find him," she promised Cody not for the first time—or the second or third. "I can feel it."

He looked at her, a trace of wonder in his expression. "How do you do it?" Cody asked.

"'It'?" Skylar questioned, not really sure what he was asking.

"How do you manage to stay so upbeat?"

"Positive thoughts," she attested. Finishing the little bit that was in her cup, she rose. "I'm going to make us some breakfast and then get ready. One of my brothers managed to find some witnesses for us to talk to," she told him.

This was all news to him, Cody thought. "When?"

"He texted me about it last night. We're going to be talking to them—separately—first thing this morning. There are two of them, both women. He might be able to find more."

"Why didn't you tell me when you got the call?" he asked.

"Simple. I wanted you to get some sleep." Opening the refrigerator, she began taking out the necessary ingredients for a typical breakfast. "If I had told you when he called me, you would have wanted to go and get started on the interviews right away. This way, you got a little bit of rest," she told him. "In my opinion," she said fondly, "you earned it."

"You're looking out for me," Cody commented.

"Someone has to," she told him, then ruffled his hair affectionately. "Go, get ready. Breakfast will be ready and on the table by the time you're finished dressing."

Cody pushed up from the table and kissed her before he went upstairs to take his shower. His manner silently told Skylar that he wasn't taking any of this for granted.

His hair was still wet when he returned to the kitchen and sat opposite her at the table.

"You got ready really quick," Skylar noted, impressed.

"I could smell the bacon frying all the way upstairs. Fastest way known to man to convince said man to come to the table," Cody told her, amused.

"And here I thought the draw was my sexy clothing," she said, pretending to pout.

Cody nodded, displaying a wicked grin. "There's that, too," he agreed. "Except in your case."

Skylar had just started to get up. That stopped her. "Oh?"

"Yes, in your case, no clothing does a far better job in luring me than sexy clothing does," he told her.

She pressed her lips together. "I'll have to remember that."

"Don't worry," Cody assured her, his voice filled with promise. "I will be sure to remind you."

That same warm shiver she was becoming increasingly familiar with slithered up and down her spine quickly. Skylar more than fondly welcomed it.

"Give me ten minutes in the shower," she requested.

"Ten minutes for a shower." Cody shook his head in absolute wonder. "You have to be the fastest woman I've ever known when it comes to getting ready," he told her. "Go, get ready—" he waved her off "—I'll take care of the dishes." He saw the laughter in her eyes. "What?"

"Oh, nothing. It's just that you're coming along very nicely," she said with a laugh.

Cody thought of the way they had made love last night. There was no real way to quite put it into words, but there was something about her that was making him feel as if he was finally turning into a real human being.

It felt good, he thought.

"Yeah," Cody said, smiling at her. "Right back at you."

Katie Lopez was the second person they'd talked to this morning. She was a young woman of about nineteen, possibly twenty, although that was probably a stretch. She was looking at them with the saddest eyes that Cody could remember ever having seen.

After he and Skylar had introduced themselves to the young woman, she told them a story that was becoming all too familiar. Certainly one that they had heard over and over again.

Masterson had befriended her, she told the duo, making her feel as if she wasn't some impossibly ugly duckling, but a desirable young woman. She admitted to fairly glowing in the his presence, ready to do anything for the handsome, rugged man paying such undivided attention to her, making her feel as if she was the very center of his universe.

That was why, when he'd made love to her, Katie hadn't paid any attention to using any method of birth control and why, when she'd gotten pregnant, he had talked her into giving up the child she hadn't been prepared—or wanted—to raise.

Until she'd suddenly felt that she changed her mind.

But he had a way with words, a way with making her do what he wanted her to do, without using a single ounce of persuasion.

"Brent said it was perfectly normal to feel the way I did." The laugh that escaped Katie's lips had an exceedingly bitter sound to it.

She continued talking. "The baby was part of me and I was just feeling her absence. He said I'd 'get over it.' He told me I just needed a break from everything—including him. So he left," she concluded.

Katie searched their faces, trying to make them see what she was feeling. "That was almost a month ago," she sighed. "I'm not feeling any better. If anything," the young woman admitted, looking from Cody to Skylar sitting next to one another in her tiny rented, furnished apartment, "I'm feeling worse."

Katie looked down at her stomach, which she still cupped protectively even though there was nothing there any longer. "It's like a huge chunk of me is missing."

There were tears in the young woman's eyes, falling freely right now. "I know this is foolish and I should have gotten over this by now, but I just can't seem to get past it.

"He said he loved me," Katie cried. "He *acted* like he loved me," she insisted. "How could he just walk away from me like that?"

"Sometimes people are just this huge lump of self-absorbed scum," Cody told the young woman. "They're just focused exclusively on what they want and, when they get that—whatever 'that' is—they just move on."

Cody looked at the unhappy young woman. "I promise you that it has *nothing* to do with you," he assured her. "It's just their own lack of character."

"Take it from me, you're a lot better off without him," Skylar stated.

"But my baby," Katie lamented. "I should have never given up my baby."

"He puts them up for adoption, doesn't he?" Cody asked.

Katie nodded her head. "That's what he said, but I don't know who he gave her to. I have no documents. He told me he would take care of everything—but he didn't," Katie moaned.

Skylar frowned, trying to connect the dots. "You didn't marry him, did you?"

"No," Katie answered sadly, like not marrying him was her biggest regret.

"We're going to do our best to track your baby down for you," Cody promised.

Stricken, Katie nodded, beginning to weep uncontrollably.

It took them a while of talking and consoling before they were able to leave Katie on her own and walk out of the woman's tiny apartment. They sat on a bench to go through the details of the interview. For what seemed like hours, they analyzed Katie's words and demeanor.

"At least Masterson left her alive," Cody commented.

"Ordinarily, I'd agree with you, but she looks as if she's really having trouble coping with this whole situation. A lot of new mothers experience postpartum depression. Sometimes it's just a mild case. Other times, the experience can be overwhelming. This woman doesn't even have a baby to show for it, which makes it exceedingly difficult for the new mother. I think Katie falls into that category. Maybe we can have her doctor recommend someone she can talk to and focus on getting better."

Skylar heard her cell phone ring. She sighed. After this last interview, she didn't feel up to dealing with another bereft young mother. They seemed to be coming out of the woodwork.

But the voice on the other end belonged to Valri.

"Take a look at your monitor," the computer expert advised her. "Looks like Mr. Romance is at it again," she told Skylar.

"You're kidding," Skylar cried.

Out of the corner of her eye, Skylar saw Cody looking quizzically at her.

"Not something I'd kid about, Sky," Valri said grimly.

"Call whichever one of my brothers is on duty, give him the coordinates at the lake and tell him that he needs to grab one of my other brothers and get there as soon as humanly possible. It's an emergency," she insisted. "Cody and I are on our way," she promised. "And thank you!" she added enthusiastically.

"I live to serve," Valri told Skylar. "I'm hanging up now." But she hadn't needed to say that. Valri found herself talking to a dial tone. Skylar had disconnected her cell phone. She and Cody were already on their way to the lake.

Chapter 25

Skylar fairly flew to the lake where the collection of cameras had been suspended, capturing different views of the area. She hadn't turned on her siren because she hadn't wanted to alert Masterson that they were on their way and scare the man away.

Because this had become a complete group effort, Skylar and Cody had several detectives staked out along the perimeter to prevent anything from going wrong.

Their main intent was to catch Masterson in the act: stealing a baby from yet another gullible young woman who had surrendered her free will to Masterson. The police detectives positioned through the area had absolutely no intention of allowing the situation to escalate and certainly no intention of letting it become dangerous.

Leaving her vehicle parked at a distance from the lake, Skylar and Cody made their way quickly toward the sound of a sobbing young woman.

"This does not sound good," Skylar whispered to Cody.

"I came here with you because I thought you wanted to talk," the crying young woman—Katie Lopez—told Masterson. Katie sounded absolutely pathetic as she sobbed. "I was hoping I could change your mind about keeping my baby. I know I said I couldn't take care of her and wanted to give her up, but I've changed my mind," Katie insisted. "Once I saw her, she just burrowed her way right into my heart. I don't want you giving her to those people who said they could take care of her." Katie wiped the tears from her eyes.

The exchange was definitely getting to Cody. The deputy was reliving what his sister had to have gone through before she'd been murdered. Skylar totally sympathized, but she really hoped that Cody could hold on to his temper before it got the better of him.

"Oh, Katie, that's what you say now," Masterson was saying. "But if you actually cared about that tiny baby, you'd see that this is the best thing you could do for her. She deserves parents who can give her the kind of life she needs, not a parent who selfishly makes decisions based on what *she* wants."

Masterson's tone had turned ugly. Skylar fought

the urge to punch the man out. He might be good-looking and silver-tongued, but he had a black, empty soul.

The girl's heartbroken sobbing mingled with the sound of the baby that she was holding in her arms.

Infuriated, Skylar looked at Cody. She could guess what he had to be going through. "Enough is enough," she whispered to the deputy. "Let's go." Beckoning him forward, she walked out into the area that surrounded the lake. The lake that had already seen at least three young women meet their demise there.

Surprised at hearing the unfamiliar voices, Masterson looked at the approaching couple. "Can I help you?" he asked with just a trace of annoyance evident in his voice as he directed his question toward Skylar. It was obvious that Masterson felt he had always had better luck with women than with men. "This *is* a private conversation," he informed Skylar.

Skylar had no desire to play this game with Masterson. "No, it's not. This young woman doesn't want to give up her baby—and no matter what you're thinking, you have no right to take this baby from her."

"You're wrong." Masterson all but spat the words, losing his patience. "I'm the baby's father."

"Being the baby's father doesn't automatically give you the right to sell that baby—or any child—to the highest bidder," Cody snapped angrily.

Feeling cornered, Masterson's face darkened. "You don't know what you're talking about."

"Oh, but I do," Cody informed the man coldly. "And a veritable *ton* of DNA found in at least three crime scenes can be used against you. I suggest that you spare yourself—and this young woman—a lot of agony, and just confess what you've done."

"I have no idea what you're talking about," Masterson snapped.

"Oh, but you do. You know exactly what we're talking about. Are you going to end this saga by coming off like a liar and a coward in this girl's eyes?" Cody asked.

Horrified, Katie instantly came to Masterson's defense. "You can't talk to him like that!" she cried.

Disgusted by the lack of backbone she had just witnessed, Skylar shook her head. "Oh, there are none so blind as those who refuse to see," she murmured under her breath.

"Open your eyes, Katie. Your so-called lover currently makes a living by impregnating young women who fall all over themselves to get his attention, then he sells those babies to couples who are desperate to adopt and who, for one reason or another, aren't able to meet the agencies' requirements."

The look on Masterson's face indicated that he felt they were much too close to the truth for his liking. Desperate, Masterson turned on the charm that had stood him in such good stead all this time.

"Look, can't we come to some sort of an agreement?" Masterson asked. Putting his hand into his pocket, he pulled out a wad of bills and waved it in front of Cody.

"Put that away before I stuff it down your throat," Cody growled angrily.

"A simple no would have done," Masterson informed him haughtily.

"You don't strike me as someone who would take no for an answer," Cody told the man.

"You're right," Masterson agreed. "I'm going to need to work on that."

"Prison would be a great place to work on that," Cody pointed out. His eyes narrowed as he ordered, "Turn around." With that, the deputy produced a pair of handcuffs and snapped them on the indignant Masterson's wrists.

Suddenly infuriated, Masterson tried—unsuccessfully—to pull away. "Is this really necessary?"

"I'm sure all the young women you killed asked that very same question," Cody told him, disgust vibrating in his voice.

"Look, maybe you and I can come to some sort of an understanding," Masterson suggested again, giving bribery one last attempt.

"Not in this lifetime," Cody informed him coldly. By that time, several detectives had surrounded them, joining their circle, which continued to grow.

Then, before either he or Skylar, or any of the others realized what was happening, Cody heard a rustling noise and felt himself being shoved aside.

It was then that he saw the raised arm. Before he or Skylar could stop it, a syringe was being plunged into the side of Masterson's neck. Caught by surprise, Masterson screamed.

"Not another move," Skylar warned. Closest to the perpetrator, Skylar grabbed the woman's wrist, knocking the now empty syringe out of her hand and sending it flying to the ground.

"He doesn't deserve to live!" the young woman who had just materialized on the scene cried. "He tried to do the same thing to me. He tried to use that kind of syringe on me because I wouldn't give up my baby. I saw him fill it with fentanyl, but I managed to knock it away and escape."

Cody knelt beside the body, but he couldn't rouse Masterson, or find the man's pulse. The fentanyl had done its job.

"He's dead," Cody finally pronounced.

The woman looked down at the dead man's body. She appeared beyond pleased. "I'm glad he's dead. He won't be able to get another young woman to do those terrible things he ordered, or to give up her baby," the young woman, Jean, declared, sobbing.

"She has a point," Cody said as Skylar's brothers, their guns drawn, gathered around the body on the ground. They were leaving nothing to chance.

"While I can't come right out and condone what this woman just did, I can totally understand why she did it. Carrie's avenged," he said, letting out a long, relieved breath. "And there's no telling how many people the woman's impetuous act just saved from having their life completely ruined."

Skylar sighed and then nodded. "I'm just glad that this whole thing is finally behind us," she commented.

Cody was more concerned with something else. "What are they going to do to her?" he asked, nodding at Jean.

"Most likely, considering what she has gone through," Skylar speculated, "she'll be placed under psychiatric care until she's deemed well enough to be able to stand trial."

Cody rolled that over in his head. "She's going to need decent representation. Maybe I can get up a collection for her." Cody debated. He sounded more than willing to do just that.

Watching Masterson's body being loaded into an ambulance, Skylar put her hand on Cody's arm. "No need to take up a collection," she told him. "I have a cousin who can defend her."

Cody laughed dryly. "Why doesn't that surprise me? You Cavanaughs seem to have people around to use for a variety of different occasions."

Skylar smiled at him. "We like being prepared for all sorts of things," she told Cody.

The deputy looked rather impressed by her statement. "Good philosophy to have," Cody said.

"Hey," Skylar's brother Finley called out, joining the duo and slinging one arm around each of their shoulders, just as another one of Skylar's brothers, Murdoch, came up behind them. "I just heard the good news. That you two managed to solve this case. Congratulations!" he declared. "You've just given Uncle Andrew his next excuse to host another family gathering. Nothing makes him happier than celebrating a killer being stopped in his tracks." Murdoch looked closely at Cody. "Speaking of which, you don't look very happy about this. Something wrong?" Murdoch asked.

"Well, I'm glad the guy's killing spree is over, but I would have rather had him stand trial and be sent to prison to serve time for doing away with so many young women—not to mention stealing and selling those babies he's responsible for creating."

"None of that would have come to light if it hadn't been for your sister's death," Skylar pointed out.

Cody frowned and shook his head, apparently not taking any of that to heart.

Skylar wasn't about to let him dwell on the down side.

"Just look at the positive side," Skylar stressed. "There might be a lot more dead women around in the future if it hadn't been for your sister bringing all this to light. You have to be able to find that to be comforting—at least to some degree."

"Oh, I do. I do," Cody told her, although there was no conviction in his voice.

Skylar's eyes swept over him as they walked back to her Crown Victoria. "You'll forgive me but, to me, you don't exactly look like a man who's been comforted," she told Cody.

"Well, that's because I just realized that this chapter is finally over. Not only that, but there's nothing really left for me back in Kiowa." Getting in the vehicle, he settled into the passenger seat. He had been dreading thinking about this point. "My parents are gone, my sister's gone—I'm having her cremated so I can have her ashes scattered here. And after working in Aurora, that little town in New Mexico seems much too tame to me."

Cody considered the situation he was faced with. It wasn't his habit to ask questions like this, but he felt as if he didn't have a choice. Not if he wanted to be around Skylar. He was at the point where he wanted to see where this relationship between them could go.

"Are there any job openings in Aurora?" he asked, doing his best to sound nonchalant.

Skylar felt her heart leap up and practically lodge in her chest.

Her eyes swept over his face. "There are *always* job openings in Aurora—if you're talking about law enforcement."

"I am," Cody confirmed, humor playing along the corners of his mouth.

She was hoping that was what he had meant. "I can fast-track your application to the police department if you like. I might not have mentioned it," she teased him, "but I know several people in a position of authority that you might like meeting and who might be able to hook you up to the department of your choice."

A grin played on his lips. "I vaguely remember you mentioning something to that effect," he told her. "I'd appreciate any recommendation you might be able to give me."

Her eyes gleamed. "Consider yourself recommended," she told him. "In addition, my uncle Brian, the Chief of Ds, has taken a special interest in you ever since you turned up on his radar."

"How far does his radar extend?" Cody asked.

She read between the lines. "Far," she assured him. "And in case you're wondering—the man does not see through walls."

"I wasn't worried about that," Cody told her.

Just then, Fin hurried over to Skylar's car and knocked on the door before she could head for the main road. She stopped driving and looked at her brother quizzically. "Anything wrong?" Skylar asked.

"On the contrary. Uncle Shane just called this in," Fin said, mentioning the head of the CSI department, "and word just reached Uncle Andrew." He looked beyond Skylar at Cody. "He'd like you to be the guest of honor at the family gathering he's planning on holding this weekend. You are going to be staying until then, aren't you?" Fin asked.

Cody exchanged glances with Skylar. "I plan to be staying a lot longer than that."

The latter nodded his approval. "Good. To put it in my uncle's words, 'Aurora could use a good man like you,'" Finley said. "And so could my sister," he added with a wide grin.

"I'll have to ask her myself," Cody said just as Skylar pulled away from the site.

Skylar was quiet for as long as she could be, then finally had to ask. "Are you? Going to ask me?" she completed.

"If *you* have to ask me that," Cody told her, "then

you're not nearly as good a detective as I thought you were."

Her eyes caught his. "Oh, I am," she told him with conviction. "I am. Tell you what. Why don't we go to my place and talk about this?" she told him.

"Perfect ending to a perfect day," Cody declared.

Her eyes teased him. "Not yet," she said, referring to the idea about it being the perfect ending to a perfect day. "But it will be," she promised.

Anticipating what was to come, Cody's face lit up. "Drive faster, Detective. Drive faster," Cody urged.

Skylar spared him an amused glance. "Remember, anything good is worth waiting for."

"Amen to that, Sky. Amen to that."

She merely smiled in agreement—and pressed down on the gas, anticipating the night that lay ahead of them.

* * * * *

COMING NEXT MONTH FROM

HARLEQUIN

ROMANTIC SUSPENSE

#2203 SHIELDING COLTON'S WITNESS
The Coltons of Colorado • by Linda O. Johnston

US marshal Alexa Colton is assigned to take care of Dane Beaulieu, a vice detective testifying against his partner's murder by a corrupt police chief. Their nine-hour drive becomes a many days' journey as they elude attackers who want them both dead. Despite escalating danger, the chemistry sizzles between them!

#2204 KILLER IN THE HEARTLAND
The Scarecrow Murders • by Carla Cassidy

When widower Lucas Maddox needs a nanny for his three-year-old daughter, he hires local woman Mary Curtis for the job. As they grow closer, Mary is threatened by a mysterious person and murders begin occurring in the small town. Lucas is determined to protect her, but can he let go of the past that holds him hostage?

#2205 HIS CHRISTMAS GUARDIAN
Runaway Ranch • by Cindy Dees

Ex-SEAL and holiday hater Nicholas Kane is no saint. But he and sexy CIA agent Alexander Creed must find a priceless nativity crèche his boss stole and return it before Christmas. Between double-crossings, rogue agents and their own guarded hearts, these spies will need a holiday miracle to find love—and survive!

#2206 SIX DAYS TO LIVE
by Lisa Dodson

It took sixty days for Dr. Marena Dash to fall in love with ex-soldier Coulter McKendrick, who's been injected with a lethal poison, but if she doesn't find an antidote, she'll lose him in six! After a bitter breakup and time apart, he shows up on her doorstep near death and with a trail of people wanting him silenced. Can Marena find the medicine he needs before the clock runs out?

YOU CAN FIND MORE INFORMATION ON UPCOMING HARLEQUIN TITLES, FREE EXCERPTS AND MORE AT HARLEQUIN.COM.

HRSCNM0922

Alex blinked, startled. This man had already done 80 percent of his job for him? Cool. All that was left now, then, was for him to finish investigating Gray and kill him.

Nick was speaking. "...got to New York City, I got lucky. I texted a guy who was brought in for some training with me about a year back. He was being groomed to take a spot on the personal security team. At any rate, he didn't answer my text, but his phone pinged as being in Manhattan. I tracked it to a restaurant and spotted Gray having supper there. I've been on his tail ever since. At least, until you knocked me off him."

"In other words," Alex said, "we need to hightail it over to wherever Gray is bunking down tonight and pick him up before he leaves in the morning."

"If we were working together, it would go something like that," Nick said cautiously.

"Seems to me we're both working toward the same goal. We both want to know what Gray stole. Why not cooperate?" In his own mind, Alex added silently, *And it would have the added benefit of me keeping an eye on you until I figure out just what your role in all of this is.*

Nick nodded readily enough and said a shade too enthusiastically, "That's not a half-bad idea."

Alex snorted to himself. Nick had obviously had the exact same thought—that by running around together, he could keep an eye on Alex, too.

If Nick had, in fact, been pulling a one-man surveillance op for the past week, he had to be dead tired. With nobody to trade off shifts with him, he'd undoubtedly been operating on only short catnaps and practically no sleep for seven days. Which made the fight he'd put up when they met that much more impressive. Alex made a mental note never to tangle with this man in a dark alley when he was fully rested.

Don't miss
His Christmas Guardian *by Cindy Dees,*
available November 2022 wherever
Harlequin Romantic Suspense books and
ebooks are sold.

Harlequin.com